WHY CAN'T YOU SEE ME?

SHADOWBOUND SERIES **BOOK ONE**

DarkRoyalty Books

KIA VALCENT

ACKNOWLEDGMENTS

Words cannot express my gratitude to all the individuals who have supported me in making this possible. First, I would like to give thanks to my mother A. Valcent for her continuous and unwavering encouragement of me, turning my passion for writing into something more. Immense gratitude goes to my favorite sister K. Valcent for her massive support, reading the final manuscript to spot unseen errors and giving me advice on the book covers and blurbs. I am eternally grateful to C. Harlow for his continuous support in helping me get what I needed done to make being an author possible. The biggest thanks go to the light of my life, my daughter ***KIA Valcent*** for giving me much love and motivation without realizing she is the one who drives me the most to succeed.

Writing has always been a burning passion of mine since I was a child and I had never imagined being an author. Being easily inspired to write a novel/novella and having to put those ideas down on paper is not as easy as it sounds and it can sometimes be overwhelming and challenging, but in the end, it is all worth it with the reward of having some individuals read your work, voice their love for it and enjoyment of reading it is what I look forward to the most.

.

SYMBOLS WITHIN THE BOOK AND THEIR MEANINGS

NAME	name of the character telling the story from their point of view
…✵…	change in character point of view
➺…	later scene, time skip/flash back/
…	new scene location
…	phone conversation scene
‡…	text messaging scene
…⃠…	beginning/ending of intimate scene

Table of Contents

CHAPTER ONE

YOU SEE ME

AXIEL

As I sat in the back of the class away from prying eyes and unwanted attention, I stared out of the classroom window, my eyes heaving with sleep as I struggled to stay awake as the teacher droned on about quantitative literacy. A reason I enjoy choosing this seat is because I get to take in the ocean's view far beyond the hills of Old Matra. When my parents told me that my homeschool teacher was moving away, and they would be sending me to public school for the last two years of high school. They wanted me to experience the normal teenage years of high school and my teacher getting married and moving away was the perfect opportunity for it to happen. Still, I never knew that spending my days in the confinement of a classroom with other students—some who barely cared and made an effort to be educated would be so suffocating.

A few days after I was told the news, and my parents went away, I watched many movies about high school life to prepare myself for what it would be like, but those movies were of no help as the experience was nothing like it looked in the movies. I tried making a few friends but nobody paid any attention to me, I thought I would make a few friends who shared the same interests as me but it's like they had a grudge against me without knowing me—at least now I know why some people went through high school with their heads down and in their books and their mind on getting into their dream college or the one their parents chose for them to attend.

After my first year, they suggested homeschooling again, since I never brought a friend home, but I vehemently refused. Sure, school was dull, but at least it provided an escape from the smothering confines of my home. Morita was my private teacher since I was a kid and I don't think I would ever be able to have the bond I had with her with anyone else and I have a feeling that if I tried a little harder, I could make a friend or two. Another reason I didn't want to go back to being taught at home was that I have a crush on the most beautiful girl in school—it felt like love at first sight and seeing her every day was my main reason for tolerating all of this. Seeing her, and potentially, in the near future, being with her is what kept me wanting to come back here. Although I haven't been able to stammer up the courage to approach her, I soon will.

Roaming the halls of Cardale Heights High School, Rejanae Ambers exuded an aura of popularity, grace, and unattainable beauty. Just being near her was like a shot of adrenaline, causing my heart to race like a sprinter, however in a school where social hierarchies were as rigid as the brick walls enclosing it, to her, I was nothing more than a ghost, blending into the sea of other students.

Just as my mind drifted into the realm of fantasy, a familiar voice jolted me back to the present. Her voice, sweet and melodic, echoed through the room, filling it with a sense of hope and comfort. Glancing up, I locked eyes with Rejanae. In that fleeting moment, her gaze revealed a blend of curiosity and uncertainty before she averted her eyes with a shy yet flirtatious smile. With my heart pounding and adrenaline pumping, her lips drew nearer, aching for the connection with mine—moments like these made the monotonous routine of school somewhat tolerable.

The blaring sound of the bell echoed through the classroom, jolting me out of my fantasy dream and back to reality. I berated myself for my inability to separate my fantasies from reality, and the consequences were becoming painfully clear. If things had advanced and class had not been dismissed, the thought of facing everyone would have been too daunting—I would then be well known to all who've never seen me.

"Of course, I was daydreaming," I sighed, my mind lost in a hazy reverie.

"Make sure you revise your work this weekend," the teacher reminded the students firmly. Her voice carried a sense of urgency as she stressed the significance of the upcoming practical exams. "None of you should have to repeat this year, especially not you, Cody!" she shouted, her voice echoing through the classroom.

"Don't worry, I won't be back," he said dismissively, brushing her off, before hastily rushing to meet up with his friends who had already exited.

I closed my notebooks, pushed my chair back, and grabbed my backpack. Looking up, I saw that most of the other students had already left, prompting me to quickly collect the rest of my things and make my way towards the exit. I was determined to reach Rejanae's locker before she did, so I could slip my note into it in time. With April underway and exams and graduation just a few months away, I found myself hopeful that she would be my prom date. Whenever I think about it, one thing that brings a smile to my face is the memory of us embarking on our college journey together.

With each step down the hallway toward her locker, my mind wandered to Rejanae once more—the way her smile could brighten even the gloomiest day, the melodic sound of her laughter echoing in my ears, the twinkle in her sky-blue eyes that held a world of wonder. Despite my countless attempts to approach her, I was always thwarted before I could speak to her. But today, she will finally acknowledge my presence.

Looking around and being as stealthy as I could, I quickly slipped a note I had written last night confessing my love to her into her locker and quickly made my way back to mine, which was only four lockers away from hers.

"Watch where you're going loser!" said Britney, shoving me against the lockers hard enough to have it make a loud thud. "Reja, hurry up or we're going to be late!"

"I'm coming, I'm coming!" she replied as she rushed past me.

She then opened her locker in a rush, causing the note I had pushed into the cress for her to fall to the ground. Being in a hurry to whatever their lunch period agenda was, she didn't even notice when the note fell to her feet. I watched, defeated, as Kelly told her a joke and they all laughed as she closed the locker and walked away. With a deep sigh, I took a long inhale before stooping to retrieve it, feeling its sharp, stabbing texture crumble in my hand.

"Seriously, she didn't see it?" I questioned myself, sighing, "I feel like I've tried everything, when will she notice me? When will she realize I exist?"

Just as I was lost in my thoughts, someone cleared their throat behind me, startling me. "Have you tried speaking to her?" a gentle voice chimed in, lacking any trace of concern.

I turned around to the voice of the question and found myself face-to-face with a girl who looked to be around my age. She stood a few inches shorter than my 6ft2 height, dressed in a black sweater adorned with white vines, black leggings under a baby blue skirt, and completed her outfit with cream ankle boots. Her gaze locked with mine as I looked down at her, taking in the sight of her long coal-black hair elegantly braided to one side over her shoulder, with bangs cascading down, roughly concealing her glasses.

Shocked, I questioned, with a light chuckle escaping my lips. "You can see me?"

Adjusting her glasses to make sure they were on her face properly, she was slightly confused by my question. With a playful tone, she responded, "Of course I can see you. You're not a ghost, nor are you invisible, ya know."

Laughing lightly, I introduced myself to her, "Axiel… and you are?" I extended my hand, ready to shake hers in a friendly gesture.

Her lip twisted in hesitation before she finally gave her response. "Vyolette," she replied, her voice hesitant as she extended her hand to shake mine. As her hand touched mine, I immediately felt a palpable, pulsating sensation course within me.

In an instant, she let go, leaving me to gaze at my palm, attempting to make sense of what had just happened. "Are… are you new?" I asked with curiosity, rubbing my fingers, still feeling the shock lingering at the tip.

"No..." she answered, her tone filled with a hint of resignation. "I just had my locker changed. I was tired of constantly being bullied at my old one, ya know?"

It's surprising that she still experiences bullying at this school, even after the board implemented a zero-tolerance policy last year. It was evident that a select few students could bypass repercussions by having their parents pay the principal a fee in exchange for silence and turning a blind eye. Vyolette asked me if she could use her locker and gestured toward the one adjacent to mine, the one I was standing in front of. I swiftly apologized and moved aside, intrigued, as I watched her input her combination and unlock her locker.

"Soooo..." I cleared my throat

"So what?" With furrowed brows, she turned toward me and asked, her tone of voice shifting abruptly. "What do you want?"

Smiling down at her, I marveled at the fact that she's been the most talkative companion I've had since I started coming here. "Uh... would you like to have lunch with me?" I asked nervously, my voice trembling slightly.

She looks at me with a puzzled expression, as if lost in deep contemplation. In moments like these, I often find myself yearning to possess the ability to read people's thoughts. However, if such a power were within my reach, I would undoubtedly direct my attention towards Rejanae.

As I awaited her response, some unwanted muttering reached my ear. "Is that guy seriously talking to the freak?" A girl's whisper was barely audible as she asked, "Has he not heard about her?"

"Who is he anyway...?" Her friend shared her opinion, saying, "They both look like freaks to me, don't you think?"

With a loud thud, Vyolette slams her locker shut, I can feel the tension in the air, and she walks away from me without a word. Curiosity filled my mind as I wondered who she was and why the girls referred to her as a freak—she seemed just like any other normal high school girl to me. Ignoring the incessant chatter of the girls, I found myself inexplicably compelled to pursue Vyolette, finding her in the back of the school sitting under a tilia cordata, shading her as she folded her knees under her, her head buried in them, and her body spasming slightly.

Silently closing in on her, an inexplicable urge to ensure her safety took hold of me, despite our unfamiliarity. It was as if my body was being controlled by an external force, guiding me towards her, guiding me to console her. I couldn't quite explain it, but a deep longing to be there for her, to be by her side, consumed me.

"Uh... hi... Vyolette," I called, concerned as I inched closer to her with caution, "are you okay?"

Startled by the depth of my voice, she quickly wiped away her tears and turned away from me, muttering that she was okay and was used to other students talking about her in such a manner.

When she turns to face me again, I suddenly spot something that was once concealed behind her long bangs and glasses, something that had gone unnoticed until now. "Y-your eyes!" I gasped, my breath catching in my throat. With a quick swipe to dry her tears, she fumbles for her glasses and puts them on, and I'm surprised to find that her eyes have inexplicably changed to a different hue.

"I'm sorry," she said, "but my vision is blurry without my glasses."

"Your eyes..." I repeated, my words coming out in a stunned whisper.

She shifted her body to face away from me as she diverted her gaze. "I know my eyes are unusual," she replied with a sigh, acknowledging their peculiarity. "They're ugly, weird—"

"No," I protested, "they're incredibly beautiful! I've never seen such a beautiful pair of eyes in my life."

She finally made her eyes meet mine. "You… you really think so…" she questioned, her words trailing, "no one has ever complimented my eyes like that before."

She smiled at me genuinely, her eyes sparkling with a newfound confidence from the unexpected compliment. I took a seat beside her without invitation, and my curiosity got the best of me as I asked why her eyes lost their vibrant violet hue and turned into a muted gray when she donned her glasses. Avoiding eye contact and brushing off my question, it was clear she had no interest in discussing it with me and I had no intention of forcing a response out of her.

We sat in silence for a moment, and I absentmindedly watched the students darting around the tracks, as well as the other sitting on the bleachers conversing amongst themselves. "Aren't you gonna go for lunch?" Vyolette asked, seeking a reason to get rid of me.

"Truth be told, I'd like to spend this lunch period with you," I answered, "if you don't mind, that is,"

With a narrowed gaze and stared at me with suspicion before she responded, "Suit yourself."

Retrieving a book from her bag and leaning against the tree to read in peaceful silence, I scooted a little closer to her and rested my back against the trunk of the tree. As we sat quietly under the tree in silence, I discreetly stole a peek at her, straining to discern the color of her eyes concealed by the frames of her glasses. They are truly beautiful, is it natural or even normal for people to have such colored eyes?

Back in class, my inability to concentrate was only amplified by the persistent rumbling in my stomach. That was the first time I skipped lunch, and until I sat down for class, my stomach didn't start growling. The sound of the last school bell echoed through the classes and halls, prompting me to swiftly pack my bag and embark on a mission to find Vyolette before she left, my thoughts consumed by her, leaving no room for my usual routine involving Rejanae. It bothered me we weren't in the same class—however, I hadn't even known she existed until today. Swimming through the sea of students who were desperate to escape the school didn't help in my quest and after I could not find her in the halls or near her locker, I waited near the school gate, hoping to see her before she left.

A sudden pulse ran through me, causing me to look up and notice Vyolette approaching, her head lowered. Ignoring my existence, she briskly walked past me, prompting me to shout her name to catch her attention. She blatantly ignored me, and when I followed closely behind her, calling her name, she took a glance back, acknowledging me for a second before looking forward and walking away again.

Irritated, she groaned in frustration. "Why do you keep following me?" she asked with a sharp edge in her voice.

I adjusted my backpack over my shoulder while trying to keep up with her. "I—I thought you might want to hang out after school," I replied, "grab a bite to eat maybe… like friends?"

With an exasperated sigh, she came to a halt and spun around to confront me, her annoyance palpable. "So, you think because you spoke to me for the first time this morning and kept me company during lunch, we're friends?" she questioned

I locked eyes with her, my mind a jumble of confusion as I desperately searched for the right words to say. "It's hard to explain," I stammered, "but for some reason, I genuinely want to be close to you—I want us to be friends."

She scoffed, her arms folding tightly under her breasts, her voice dripping with skepticism. "Yeah right, like you won't just humiliate me when I least expect it. I've been at this school for almost five years and I have been tricked enough times to know when someone has it out to humiliate me, nobody wants to be friends with a freak!"

"What? Why would I do that?" I asked, my voice filled with bewilderment.

A small crowd formed around us, and the students gathered began calling out for others to come watch the bickering freaks. I glanced around and was surprised to see them ready for a pointless drama. I questioned if this was the only thing I needed to do to get noticed at this school. Humiliated, Vyolette lowered her head, unable to meet the gazes of the gathering crowd of students, and said something under her breath. Raising her head and glaring at me with contempt, she cursed at me, demanding that I leave her alone before storming off. I felt an urge to chase after her, but I resisted and left the school premises, making my way home. With all eyes on me now, I knew for a fact that the invisibility cloak I'd had on for the last two years was now gone and I would now be the talk of the school—at least in a few months, I'll never have to come back here and face them again.

➔AT HOME

With a clouded mind, I made my way home and parked in the front, grateful that the pull I felt earlier toward Vyolette had finally subsided. The moment I swung open the front door of my home, my attention was drawn to a few suitcases, their colors standing out against the neutral backdrop—one in a bold red and the other in a serene forest green near the door.

I knew exactly what this meant, and it filled me with a sense of dread. "Mom, Dad?" I called out, my voice echoing through the grand foyer of the house, "Are you guys leaving again?"

"Axiel, honey," my mom's concerned and slightly sorrowful voice echoed through the living room as I walked in. She held onto my shoulders, her worried eyes meeting mine, as she sat me down and explained that she and my dad would be leaving for a while, leaving me alone at home.

Annoyed by her overreacting, I couldn't help but roll my eyes, which only prompted her to shake me slightly and scold me for my rudeness. They've been leaving me home alone since I was thirteen, so it's nothing new to me. "How long is a while?" I questioned, my tone lacking enthusiasm.

"Six months to a year," she replied, her voice fading away as she let go, leaving a sense of ambiguity in the air.

My eyes grew wide, they'd never left that long before. The duration of their time away from home has varied, sometimes lasting only a week or two, other times stretching to a month or three, but it never exceeded six months to a year. "So long?" I questioned, my voice betraying me with cracks and uncertainty.

Growing up, my parents were constantly by my side, doting on me and never wanting to let me out of their sight. However, on my ninth birthday, they began traveling and for as long as I can remember, they've never been around much since then. Until I was thirteen, I was left here with a live-in nanny and tutor. However, for the past two years, they haven't left for more than a month, and I finally felt like we were truly living as a normal family again. I guess it was my mistake to expect so much from them.

"Is it a problem, sweetheart?" my mother asked, "if it is, we can call Morita to come to live with you until we get back,"

"It's not that," I quickly declined, "but if you guys are going away for that long, won't you be missing my graduation?" I asked, my voice tinged with disappointment.

Before redirecting their gazes towards me, they locked eyes with each other. "It's just a graduation Axiel," my father reassured me, "I'll have a videographer capture every moment, and we'll cherish the memories when we return."

"What?" I yelled, "It's not the same thing! You guys promised me you would attend!"

"Lower your tone Axiel," my mother said strictly as she looked up at me, "you need to understand where your father is coming from, there are more important things than a school graduation!"

"It's not just a school graduation Mom," I argued, "it's my high school graduation,"

"And I'm sure you'll have a college graduation," my father argued back, "it's not more important than the work we need to do!"

As my father grew increasingly agitated, my mother gently placed her palm on his chest, calming him. Whatever they had to travel for this time must be truly important since I've never seen my father so driven and serious before. "Honey, understand where your dad is coming from," she stated, "we're not sure how long we'll be gone but I promise you, we'll try to get it done quickly and come back as soon as we're able, promise."

Defeated, I let out a sigh and sank into the chair's plush cushions. They each took a seat beside me and rested a hand on my shoulder, "what we do is for your best interest Axiel," said my mother, "You do not know how important you are to us."

"Leaving your only son alone in an enormous house for a year is in their best interest?" I questioned sarcastically, "is that your way of showing how important I am to you guys?"

"If you only knew..." murmured my father, his voice barely audible.

"Then explain to me," I retorted, my tone sharp and cutting, clarifying that I had heard his comment.

They locked eyes one more time, then directed their focus towards me, refusing to entertain my outburst. I swear if I ever died when they're away, they'd never find out, not until they return, at least. Despite my attempts to seek a straightforward answer about their extended absence, the conversation with them remained elusive, leading me to surrender and declare that I didn't need a babysitter and would manage on my own. At eighteen years old, I consider myself practically an adult and didn't need some two-faced, thieving hag to look after me while they were away.

With everything set, and me accepting the inevitable, I walked my parents to the front door. My father carried the suitcases to his car, their wheels clacking against the pavement. Meanwhile, my mother stood on the front porch, her concerned gaze locked on me, her forehead creased with worry. It felt as if she had something important to say, but there was a barrier preventing her from sharing it. She rummaged through her handbag, searching for her purse, before finally pulling out a card and handing it to me.

"Here," she said, placing a black card in my hand. "This is yours, with no spending limit. But remember, that doesn't permit you to be careless with your purchases," she cautioned.

My father cleared his throat, his deep cough startling me, and brought his hands together with a resounding clap. "Can't believe I'm saying this," he cautioned, "but let's refrain from throwing wild parties, Axiel. It's crucial to understand that having your school or classmates over for one doesn't equate to genuine friendship."

"I've seen the movies, Dad," I responded nonchalantly, "I know,"

"Good," said my mother, her arms wrapping around me in a tight embrace. "Remember that I love you—we both love you—and everything we do is solely for your well-being."

"I understand Mom," I responded with a soft sigh, "I love you too."

Once my parents had left for the airport, I took a shower to wash away the bittersweet emotions of them shutting me out once again. I don't know what's so important about them doing archaeological spelunking for my benefit far less, my best interest. Freshened up, I made my way downstairs, hungry and in need of sustenance, since I hadn't eaten any lunch at school. With no desire to cook or wait for takeout, I opted for a quick drive downtown in my *Toyota Highlander*. I drove around for a while and while passing by a small local diner at the edge of town, I felt a familiar tug, the same one I had experienced after my encounter with Vyolette.

"What is this feeling…?"

CHAPTER TWO

I SEE YOU

VYOLETTE

It took me a full hour to walk back home, and by the time I reached my doorstep, I was utterly fatigued, yearning to crawl into bed and sleep until the sun rose again. Leaning back on the swing chair on the front porch, I closed my eyes and let the rhythmic creaking and swaying lull me into a state of introspection about the day I had. The memory of Axiel's comment made me smile, a genuine smile that contrasted sharply with the painful experiences of being humiliated by others who pretended to want to be my friend but only sought to fit in with the school's popular clique and humiliate me as an initiation.

Getting lost in such deep thoughts plunged me into a state of sadness as I recollected the seven instances where I was deceived into believing someone genuinely wanted to be my friend. The first time I thought I made a friend during my first year of high school, I was invited to a sleepover, my parents were thrilled to hear that, but when I got there, I found out that the address I was given was to an abandoned house on the edge of the next neighborhood which sent me into an unwanted spiral. The second time was during a summer camp I was forced to go to by the school counselor—I don't want to talk about that one, I was simply happy to make it home safely.

What made me completely shut myself in and not get close to anyone ever again was when I was practically kidnapped and locked in the school boiler room basement for an entire weekend. The principal stubbornly dismissed my claims, insisting that I couldn't possibly know the culprits since I was attacked from behind. My memory is a blank canvas before the accident, only starting from that moment on. I don't think my family ever had money, so I was always on the lower spectrum in school, and since the accident, I have been subjected to relentless bullying throughout my life by the other students and even some teachers. You would think after such a tragic accident, people would have a heart and just leave me alone, but it only got worse.

At that point, I questioned the purpose of my existence, wondering if I was meant to endure nothing but suffering. Three more months, and I'll never have to endure this school's hallways and classrooms and sick students ever again. When I leave this town, I will never return, I am going to go somewhere where nobody knows me, somewhere I can be myself—somewhere I would be accepted and make a genuine friend or two.

'*I want us to be friends…*'

"Axiel..." I murmured, reminiscing about his gentle gaze and how it matched the authenticity in his voice when he expressed his desire to be my friend. "Did I make a mistake? Was I too mean to him? I wouldn't be surprised if he never speaks to me again."

Struggling to read the time on my watch due to the cracked screen, I unlocked the front door and stepped inside. I immediately removed my glasses and placed them on the end table next to the entrance. "Welcome home, sweetie," said my mom, happy to see me home safely, "how was your day?"

I gave a nonchalant shrug, and my father let out a forced chuckle. "Same old, same old?" he questioned

Welcomed into their embrace, I felt a sense of comfort and joy, a familiar routine that I cherish each day when I leave for school, knowing that I will return home to the loving arms of my parents. "I've miss you guys so much," I sobbed in their arms.

"We know sweetie," said my mother, "we know, we miss you too,"

My father suddenly pulled away and stared at me at arm's length, "is everything okay puppy?" he asked, "something seems… different,"

I wiped my tears and tucked my bangs behind my ears as I looked up at them, "everything's okay," I reassured them, "though… I think I made a friend."

"A friend!" my mom exclaimed, her voice filled with excitement. "That's amazing news!"

I forced a smile and hugged her once again. It might sound great, but if he truly gets to know me, he'll run away and start bullying me just like everyone did after the accident. The weight of those past experiences lingers, leaving a bitter taste in my mouth. '*Nobody wants to be friends with a freak.*' the words of past so-called friends echoed in my mind. Wanting to make the most of my evening, I quickly brought my school bag up to my room. I then proceeded to make an early dinner for the family, as I knew that once I came back from work, all I would want to do was sleep. As we sat at the table, my parents listened intently as I narrated the entire story of my encounter with Axiel, and their expressions revealed a deep sense of happiness and gratitude that someone had shown genuine concern for me.

"Aren't you guys hungry?" I asked, eyeing their untouched plates of creamy mac and cheese.

Their eyes met, and a shared smile passed between them, but then they quickly refocused their gaze on me. "Honey..." my mother said, reaching her hand over the table to rest it on mine.

Tears streamed down my face, as I couldn't hold back my emotions. "I'm so sorry, Mom," I apologized, my eyes downcast and my tone apologetic. "I forgot again…"

"It's ok sweetie," she replied, her voice tinged with sympathy. "We're the ones who should be apologizing for making you go through this."

Despite their apologies, I still couldn't shake off the guilt for always getting carried away whenever we ate together. Feeling a mix of annoyance and impatience, I bit down on my inner lip and muttered to myself as I pushed my chair away from the table. "I'm gonna be late for work."

I excused myself and made my way up to my room to change into my work uniform. It was a knee-length, yellow button-down dress with delicate white and yellow plaid trims. As I glanced at myself in the mirror, my attention was diverted to my budget book, which lay open on the bed. I grabbed it, closed it, and tossed it on my desk before slinging my side bag over my shoulder and descending the stairs to exit the house as I had a long walk ahead of me. As much as I would love to buy a car, I can't afford one and couldn't afford to take a bus either—my way back home relied on tips. Between paying the house bills, buying groceries, and purchasing school supplies, I barely have enough money to cover my personal expenses, let alone save up for a used car.

As I prepared to leave, I embraced my parents, cherishing the feel of their arms around me. "Be cautious, my little puppy," my dad reminded me.

"I will, Dad," I said reassuringly, giving them each a kiss on the cheek. "I'll see you guys when I get back."

➛LATER AT WORK

As I arrived at work, I entered through the discreet back entrance, carefully placing my bag in my assigned locker before making my way to the bustling kitchen where the two head chefs were deep in conversation amongst themselves. As I approach, I see Monique, the manager of the diner in the corner of my eye, engaged in a conversation with one of the assistant cooks, their voices blending with the clattering of pots and pans.

"Vyolette, you're here," she greeted me warmly, her smile putting me at ease as she motioned for the assistant cook to go continue with her work.

"Hi Monique," we shared a brief hug, "I'm not late, am I?"

"In my books, you're never late, Vy," she quipped, teasing me about my perpetual lateness. "I understand how it is for you."

I clasped her hand, "I don't want sympathy for my situation, Monique," I responded, "I just want to be treated normally like everyone else!"

She giggled softly with a snort. "Aww sweetie, you're anything but normal," she stated, "now go wait on some tables," she commanded

With a sigh, I shake my head, reflecting on how my life deviated from the norm at age nine. Despite this, I find solace in her acceptance—a rare gem in a world that often fails to comprehend me. "Yes, boss!" I smiled, giving her a hefty salute.

Monique, my mother's best friend, has been like a second mother to me after my accident, always extending her invitation for me to live with her, but I'm hesitant to leave the comfort of my parents' home. I'm comfortable where I am right now and I don't think my parents would want me to go to Monique's, nor would they want to go with me and I don't think she'll be fine with it, even though she's said to me many times that it wouldn't bother her if we all came to live with her.

After taking a moment to freshen up in the washroom, I tied my hair back in a ponytail. I washed my hands before grabbing my apron, notepad, and pen, and then I headed out onto the floor to work.

"Welcome to ***Spitin-Ya Food***," I stated, after approaching my first table. "May I take your order?"

"What the heck!" exclaimed the customer, "Who came up with such a bizarre restaurant name?"

"Did you not look at the name when you entered?" I questioned with a light chuckle.

"No..." he answered, his voice trailing off, "I'm not really—"

When he looks up to meet my gaze, my eyes widen at the sight of the familiar amber-hazel eyes shining through the retro-square gold and black glasses. "Shit!" I muttered softly under my breath to myself.

"Vyolette?" Axiel gasped, combing his fingers to his arch fringe and scissor-taper hair, bringing it away from his face. "What are you doing here?"

I bit my inner lip, looking up for a moment and giving a quick prayer for tolerance before giving him my attention once again. Of the fifties and hundreds of restaurants, diners, food trucks, and food stands in this district, he chose the one I work at to come to. I've been working here for years and have never seen him here before, was he following me? One of the reasons I worked here was because it was far away from my home community and I didn't have to deal with the assholes and bitches of the school coming here to run amuck and embarrass me.

"Isn't it obvious?" I replied, making an effort to be polite while gesturing towards my work clothes.

"Well, that's obvious," he stammered, clearing his throat in minor embarrassment.

"What are you doing all the way here, anyway?" I questioned, my eyebrows furrowing in confusion.

"Well, I didn't feel like cooking or ordering takeout, so I thought I'd go for a drive and find somewhere to grab a bite," he explained, "I'm sure you could guess where I ended up."

I shook my head slightly, rolling my eyes in annoyance as I asked harshly, "What do you want to eat?"

"Oh... uh...." he stammered, looking at the menu, "I'll have fish and chips and a glass of lime juice please,"

"Coming right up..." I responded, tapping the tip of my pen on my notepad and turning around to bring his order to the chef. "Practically drove for a half hour for some fish and chip," I spoke to myself.

As I brought him his order, I couldn't help but notice the satisfied smile on his face when he looked at me, which motivated me to continue serving the other customers with enthusiasm—taking brief glances at his table as I moved around the diner. Despite my expectations, he didn't leave once he was done eating—instead, he stayed for a while, leaving me curious if he was intentionally waiting for me to finish work.

I recalled what my parents said before I left the house and lost myself in a smile. Still, recalling that he might want to walk me home, I came back to my senses and avoided him for the rest of the night. After my shift had ended, I lingered a little longer in the back, hoping he would leave so I could avoid talking to him or him offering to walk me home.

With a smile, Monique emerged from the back room, the sound of her heels echoing through the empty room. "Got a new crush, I see?" she said, taking a seat beside me.

"Don't make a mountain out of a molehill," I replied, "He's just a guy at school whom I made the mistake of talking to. Claims he wants to be my friend, but we both know that's a lie,"

She laughed and took a seat beside me. "sweetie, the way he looks at you says he might want to be more than just friends… besides, if he wants to be your friend and get to know you Vy, then why are you pushing him away?" she questioned, ignoring my previous statement.

I groaned, "Monique, I'm weird! I'm a freak!" I cried, "Once he gets to know me, he'll just run away and call me one and start humiliating me just like everyone else did."

I felt a surge of emotion, my eyes brimming with tears, and Monique held me tightly, offering reassurance and support. I wanted to remove my glasses to wipe my tears, but this wasn't the best place or time to do so. She reassured me, her voice filled with conviction, that Axiel was different from the others who came before him. She encouraged me to trust him, to let my guard down just enough, and to allow him the opportunity to be my friend.

"It's gonna be okay Vyolette." she whispered, patting my back lightly, "Not everyone's the same, and I'm sure if you open up to him just a little, you'd see he may not be like everyone else."

"I… I don't know Monique," I whimpered

She hugged me again, rubbing my back in a comfortable gesture and threatening to hurt him if he dared hurt me in any way, a promise I knew she would keep after her reaction when I told her what happened to me last year from the last person who pretended to want to be my friend.

I collected myself, uttered my farewell, and departed swiftly, considering the last bus departed at midnight, and I couldn't risk being stranded. When I reached the bus stop, I found myself standing alone, the group of girls I used to catch the bus with were absent, which meant that I had missed the bus. When I glanced at my watch, I realized it had stopped ticking, leaving me clueless about the current time. As I walked back to the restaurant, I noticed Monique's car still parked in the side lot, so I took a seat on the bench in front and patiently waited for her to finish closing up.

"Need a lift?" Axiel asked, his voice filled with warmth and sincerity.

"SUN ANA GUN!" Startled, I leaped out of my seat and skin, my hand instinctively clutching my chest to check if my heart was in place and still beating. "What are you doing here, Axiel?"

His hands were restless in his pockets, fidgeting with the fabric. "I was worried about you," he confessed.

"Looks more like you're stalking me," I retaliated, "I served you almost seven hours ago, you should've been long gone."

"I did leave," he said, "but I was worried about you and didn't know if you had a safe way home, so I came back to make sure," he explained.

"What?" I said, "Is this some kind of joke? Why are you going out of your way to—"

"I don't know," he responded, "I just feel this—"

"Vyolette, you're still here?" Monique called from near the side of the building, "Did your friend come back to pick you up, that's great."

Using a menacing tone, she directed her words towards Axiel, warning him to take good care of me or she would deal with him accordingly. She then waved me off, leaving no room for me to respond as she got into her car, pulled out of the lot, and drove off.

With my last-ditch effort to leave the diner, I watched the red taillights fade into the darkness of the night, feeling defeated. Reluctantly, I agreed to let Axiel Walk me home. The last bus was gone, and I honestly did not want to walk home all by myself. I stood to my feet and thanked Axiel for his kindness in walking me home.

With his towering height, he looked down at me, his eyes piercing into mine. "Walk?" he questioned, his deep voice rumbling through the air. "Did you walk here?"

"Yeah," I answered honestly, "I usually get the bus back, but I guess I missed it."

Had I known he had left earlier, I would have quickly made my exit, too. He mentioned he had driven here, and I followed his lead to where his SUV was parked, just across the street from the diner. Climbing into his vehicle, we buckled our seatbelts, and with a flick of a switch, the engine sprang to life, its powerful rumble resonating through the car as we began our drive, the journey into town characterized by a tranquil silence.

"I'm glad you agreed to let me drop you home, Vyolette," he said with a soft smile.

"Didn't have much of a choice," I replied slightly sarcastically, "Monique practically abandoned me back there. I'd like to give you some gas money for your troubles."

As I opened my bag to retrieve some change from the tips I had made today, I felt my finger brush against a sharp object. In a moment of intense pain, I yanked my hand back and examined my finger, which had been unexpectedly slightly lacerated.

"What's wrong?" Axiel asked, struggling to keep his eye on the empty dark road.

"I cut myself on my knife," I responded, holding the finger with the cut.

"Let me see it," he suggested, gently pulling my hand towards him and studying it closely as blood trickled from the wound. Without warning, he swiftly sucks the blood off it, leaving behind a faint coppery scent.

"What the hell are you doing?" With a sudden motion, I withdrew my hand and slapped him, causing him to let the vehicle swerve before he regained control, the sensation of coldness lingering on my skin as the stiff wind blew against it. "Are you crazy?"

"I'm sorry," he acted contrite, his tone apologetic. "That's what my mom usually did whenever I had a cut on my hand," he confessed, his voice filled with a mix of guilt and nostalgia.

"And yet they label me as a freak?" I argued, pleadingly, "Just... take me home!" I commanded with desperation in my voice.

He apologized and then resumed driving, but as time passed, I couldn't help but notice his growing fatigue. As I stole a glance at him, I observed his ashen face and the way his eyelids drooped, signaling his impending loss of consciousness. Meanwhile, the vehicle began its erratic swaying as he struggled to maintain control of it and stay in the right lane.

"Are you feeling alright?" I asked, "Do you want me to drive?"

"It's fine," he chuckles, his laughter laced with a touch of exhaustion. "I'm just a little light-headed is all. I'll rest as soon as I get home."

As we entered my home street, I instructed him to make a right turn. He followed my directions and parked on the side of the street, the engine purring softly in neutral. "Thanks for taking me home," I said with gratitude

"This is your home?" he asked, leaning over to my side and taking in the sight of the dilapidated, deserted-looking house with overgrown grass nearly four feet tall on the front lawn.

"Yeah," I answered, "I know it—"

"It looks incredibly neglected and abandoned," he remarked, stating the obvious, "I've seen this house before, but I never imagined anyone actually living there."

"It has electricity and running water," I replied snarkily, "I'm making it work."

Sensing my annoyance, he ceased his comments and shifted his focus back to the house. "Well, at least your parents are there too," he commented, his head making a subtle nodding motion.

My breath caught in my throat as I gasped, unable to believe what I had just heard. "What did you just say?" I exclaimed.

"Your parents..." he repeated, pointing towards the porch, "Aren't those your parents standing there, waiting for you? They must be really worried to be waiting there like that at this time of the night and in this cold weather."

When I lowered my glasses and looked up, my heart skipped a beat as I saw my mom and dad standing exactly where he had said they were. Adjusting my glasses, I turned around to look at Axiel. "Leave now!" I commanded, as I swiftly exited his car.

"Wait... what?" he stammered, "Did I say something wrong? Did I do something wrong?"

"I SAID TO LEAVE!" I exploded, ignoring his questions.

"Okay, okay..." he reluctantly said with his hands raised in a gesture of compliance, "I'm leaving, have a good night."

As he drove off, I stood there, flabbergasted, the image of his car slowly shrinking in the night. "*How could he...?*"

CHAPTER THREE

SEE THE FLAMES

AXIEL

Last week, I mustered up the confidence to express my feelings to Rejanae, but her response was anything but kind. The experience is baked in my memory. *She recoiled in disgust, shouting, "Get away from me, you freak!" before shoving me away and dusting off her hand like she touched something unsanitary. "Ugh, disgusting! I'll never be interested in a loser like you!"*

"Thank you, sir, have a good night," Vyolette's voice cut through my trail of thought.

When I shared the story with Vyolette, her laughter was contagious. It hurt to see her reveling in my misery, but her response served as a stark wake-up call. Falling for someone solely based on their appearance can be quickly reshaped when you finally interact with them and discover their personality. While talking to Vyolette, I realized my feelings for Rejanae were misguided. I understood I was only infatuated with the notion of being with her, like the cliché of a nerdy schoolboy pining after the unattainable, most popular girl in school.

Since the day I met and spoke to Vyolette, nearly two weeks ago, my life has taken on a strangely meaningful quality that I can't quite explain. It took some convincing, but now she allows me to drop her off and pick her up from work and school. However, despite our growing closeness, she remains adamant about not letting me set foot inside her house.

"Talk about overdramatic!" I whispered to myself, barely audible.

"Waiting on Vyolette to complete her shift again?" Monique said, pouring me another cup of coffee.

"Hi Monique," I greeted, my smile widening, "Yes, I am."

Before joining me at my table, she glances at Vyolette, her voice lowering to a hushed whisper. "Is she still giving you a hard time?" she questioned

I was going to deny it, but every time we spoke, she seemed to have a deeper understanding of Vyolette than I did, making it easy for her to tell if I was lying. Plus, I'm a terrible liar, I couldn't tell one to save my life. "She is," I confessed, "I have a feeling she's still skeptical about me and is handling me with a fifteen-foot pole."

Monique rested her order book on the table, leaning in as if about to divulge valuable information about Vyolette. "Sweetie, you should know that Vyolette is not like other girls, she's special,"

"I know that ma'am," I admitted, "I, I can feel it whenever I'm near her and when I'm away from her… I just want to be near her—so bad sometimes it hurts,"

"I don't think you comprehend what I'm saying," she shook her head, signaling her readiness to go into more detail. "You see, Vyolette is... there's something unique about her."

"What do you mean?" I questioned, confused.

Monique began explaining herself, stealing another fleeting glance at Vyolette. "Nine years ago, Vyolette and her parents were on their way home from a carnival that was in town at the time, when they had a collision with a drunk driver," she began, "Vyolette was in a coma for a year and when she woke up, she wasn't the same,"

"I… I don't understand…" I murmured

Adjusting herself in the seat, she resumed her story. "When she woke up, she was told about the accident and had a mental breakdown, she shut her eyes so hard and screamed which caused a blast, and when she opened them, they were a dark violet, call it a panic attack, call it an outburst of being told she can't see her parents, but it took about five enormous guys to hold her down so they could sedate her, she damaged half the hospital wing—although, she has no memory of it now," she replied, taking a breath as she continued. "When she woke up again, she began screaming about seeing people who doctors and nurses said weren't there, begging to get out of the hospital… they had to sedate her so many times the doctors were ready to have her taken away to a mental asylum but her grandmother fought for her to be put in her care,"

"What do you mean?" I asked, "Seeing people that weren't there?"

"She was seeing the dead Axiel," Monique stated, "lost souls who hadn't crossed to the other side,"

"Wait, why did her grandmother fight to have her in her care, why not her parents?" I questioned, waiting for a response to ask the more important question after.

Monique sat upright, her eyes searching mine with confusion. "She didn't tell you?"

"Tell me what?" I asked

"Her parents died in the accident," she answered, "Vyolette was adamant that they weren't, and only stopped debating after she was shown a video of their funerals."

The memory of seeing her parents that first night I dropped her off resurfaced, but I thought it would be wiser not to mention it to Monique. If her parents indeed died the night of the accident, could the people I see be their ghosts? Was Vyolette living with their spirits or something? That could explain why the house looked so rundown and dilapidated, with broken windows and peeling paint.

Monique then revealed that Vyolette's grandmother had gifted her with a pair of glasses to shield Vyolette from the ethereal presence of lost souls.

"Is that why her eyes are gray when she has them on and violet when she doesn't?" I questioned

"You've seen them?" With excitement in her voice, she exclaimed, "I've never seen a more beautiful pair of eyes."

She nodded in agreement and briefly glanced at Vyolette before refocusing her attention on me. "Look, I don't know much since the conversation I was supposed to have with her mother didn't happen," she stated, "but I do know that there's more to Vyolette than just her seeing ghosts and having violet eyes—they only became violet after her accident. I'm begging you to please, not hurt her, if you can't handle being a part of her life knowing this about her, please, leave peacefully."

"Monique, as crazy as this sounds, I don't think I can ever leave her side," I confessed, "Vyolette—"

Monique's gaze shifted towards the cashier, where a clock on the wall ticked away the seconds. "We're gonna have to continue this conversation at a later date," she cut me off, "Vyolette's shift is ending soon."

Monique left the table, leaving me with a whirlwind of thoughts. If Vyolette can see the ghost of the dead, and her parents have been deceased for nearly ten years, then why did I witness them eagerly awaiting her on the front porch the very first night I dropped her at her home?

"Thanks for waiting for me Axiel," said Vyolette, as she approached me with her side bag slung over her shoulder, "are you ready to go?"

"Uh, yeah," I replied

After getting up from my table, I quietly trailed behind her as she made her way out of the diner. I stole a glance back and saw Monique waving at me with a reassuring smile, mouthing something and giving me a cutthroat gesture, before turning around and getting back to work.

→→→

The drive back to Old Matra was serene, with the windows rolled down to let in the chilly breeze, gently rustling my and Violet's hair. Although it was late—fifteen minutes to midnight—I insisted on taking in the mesmerizing sight of the ocean stretching out before us from the cliff. The moon was full and radiant, casting a shimmering reflection on the calm sea water beneath a sky adorned with countless stars, it was a breathtaking sight I longed to share with her.

As we got back on the road, the late hour became more apparent, with only a few headlights illuminating the otherwise deserted roads. Violet hummed a song in her head happily as I drove onto her street. A smile appeared on my face but quickly vanished as I spotted a bright orange light illuminating the distance, accompanied by billowing black smoke against the dark sky.

"Is there a bushfire?" she asked, leaning forward as I turned the corner.

"We don't live so close to the woods," I replied, confused, eager to know what was ablaze. "I think it might be a building on fire—"

"Oh my gawd, NO!" she screamed as we drove closer, "that's my house!"

I felt her heart sink as we neared her burning home, the blazing inferno illuminating the night sky and casting an eerie glow on the firefighters desperately battling the flames, neighbors gathered in the cold of the night on the street to see the raging flames get put out, kept at a distance by officers and barricades. Vyolette wasted no time in getting out of the vehicle. Before I could finish parking the car, she had unbuckled her seatbelt and sprinted towards the inferno. In an instant, I found myself outside of the SUV too, the acrid smell of smoke filling my nostrils as I tightly embraced her, preventing her from entering the raging fire.

Holding her back was like trying to tame a wild beast, as she screamed and thrashed, demanding to be released. "Let go of me!" she pleaded, "Mom, Dad, somebody help them, please!" Ignoring her pleas, I wrapped my fingers tightly around her stomach, ensuring a secure grip.

Seeing me struggling to hold her back, a firefighter approached us. "Is this your house, young lady?"

"It is," she cried, "did my parents make it out, are they safe?"

The firefighter stared at her, confused, shifting his gaze from her to me, then back to her. "I'm sorry?"

"My parents," she cried with tear-filled eyes, "they were in there, please tell me you got them out safely,"

"Young lady," he stated, "my men combed the house and found no one—not a soul. We thought it was abandoned until the neighbors mentioned that a young girl lived there on her own."

Her voice cracked with emotion as she gave her command, tears streaming down her cheeks. "Well, look again, because there are souls in there!"

With each thrust, she pushed her back and head against me, creating a fluctuating tension in my grip. I had to calm her down. If what Monique told me was true—that her parents are dead—the emergency personnel would label her as crazy and unstable and have her taken to a mental asylum if she can't keep her composure.

With a forceful grip on her waist, I tilted her face to meet my gaze with my other hand, locking eyes with her. "VYOLETTE LOOK AT ME!"

"NO! LET ME GO!" she screamed, her voice filled with fury and desperation, as she exerted even more force, her nails digging deeper into my skin, a painful reminder of her determination to break free. As she got angrier and more desperate to save her parents, powerful gusts of wind whipped around us, fueling the flames and causing some firefighters to lose their balance, creating a sense of an impending tornado.

I turned her around to face me, wrapping my arms tightly around her in a heartfelt embrace. "Calm down Vyolette, please!" My voice cracked as I pleaded, "You still have me," hoping my words would offer some solace. "You still have me… and I promise you I am not going anywhere… so please calm down… you still have me…"

The moment my words reached her ears, I could feel her strength evaporate, and she crumbled into my arms, her heavy sobs soaking my shirt with her tears. I allowed her to unleash her frustration on me, feeling each blow of her fists as a reflection of her inner turmoil, until we both collapsed onto the cold street, tears streaming down her face.

Her voice trembled as she whispered the words, "Mom... Dad..." before succumbing to unconsciousness.

The heavy winds ceased, and the firefighter who had been carried away earlier returned. "Is she going to be okay?" he asked anxiously, "Should I call one of the paramedics to examine her?"

"No, it's fine," I replied, "but thank you…"

He mentioned that because of the run-down condition of the house, the fire might have been caused by an electrical issue. However, the investigators would confirm the cause, and I would receive a call once they were done. I thanked him once again and informed him she could spend the night and the following days with me, and after giving me a nod of agreement, he made his way back to the house, now a charred shell, with firefighters actively working to extinguish the remaining flames. I scooped Vyolette in my arms, got to my feet, carried her back to the SUV, and strapped her in for safety.

I stood in anticipation, my eyes fixed on the fading smoke. The firefighters' efforts were commendable as they battled the last remnants of the fire. A scenario plagued my mind—had I not insisted we stop at the cliff to look at the view, she would have arrived home earlier and been in that house when it caught fire.

⇢⇢⇢

We pulled into the driveway of my Romulus modern two-story home and I used the remote to open the garage door before driving in and closing it behind me. I got out of the SUV and went over to Vyolette's side to help her out.

As I unstrapped her, she groaned, and her eyes fluttered open. "Where—where am I?" she grumbled as she wrapped her hands around my neck.

"We're at my place," I answered, "don't worry, you can stay with me as long as you need to… you're safe."

As I carried her up the stairs to the living room, my back brushed against the banister. I gently laid her down on the chair, ensuring she was comfortable, and then hurried to the kitchen to fetch a glass of ice-cold water. "Thank you," she said, taking the glass of water from me.

She takes a sip and holds the glass in her hand as she stares at it blankly. "Are you gonna be okay, Vyolette?" I inquired worriedly.

She nods solemnly, her tear-stained face reflecting the devastation of losing everything in the fire. Understandably, I don't blame her because, who knows, her parents' spirit might have been trapped in the house that's now reduced to ashes.

I held her in my arms as she cried for another hour before leading her upstairs to the guest bedroom, where she would be sleeping. Before she settled down for the night, I wanted to make sure she felt cozy and cared for. I ran a bath for her, making sure the water was just the right temperature and placed a set of towels on the counter for her to use when she was done. Since I didn't have any sisters and my parents' room was strictly off-limits, I couldn't find her something of my mother's, so I offered her my t-shirt and boxer to wear for the night.

"Tomorrow is Saturday, so we can go to the mall and I can buy you some new clothes, shoes, and anything else you will need," I said, wiping the tears from her eyes. "For tonight, you can wear the clothes I set for you on the bed."

"Okay," she mumbled

Looking up at me, she allowed me to gently brush her long bangs away, revealing her soft face. With hesitation, I carefully took off her glasses and set them on the bathroom counter, unable to tear my eyes away from the mesmerizing beauty of her violet eyes.

"Thank you, Axiel," she muttered

With a small nod, I quietly left the bathroom, allowing her to have the privacy she needed. While making my way downstairs to grab a drink, a sharp, agonizing pain gripped my chest, prompting me to rush back up to the bathroom. To my horror, I discovered Vyolette in the tub, her face stained with tears, as she unsteadily ran a blade along her wrist.

"Vyolette, what are you doing?!" I yelled, my voice echoing through the air as I rushed to her aid. Snatching the blade from her hand and throwing it across the room, I felt a brief pain as it nicked my fingers. Still, I ignored it and held her tightly against my chest.

"Let me die!" she cried, her voice filled with despair. "I have nothing left to live for! My mom and dad are gone! I'm all alone in this world now..."

I pulled her out of the tub, and as she rested her head on my chest, I could feel her sobs reverberating through her body. "You're not alone Vyolette," I reassured her, "You still have me, and I swear to you, I will never leave your side."

The moment my words reached her ears, she latched onto me, tears streaming down her face as she sobbed inconsolably. In her broken whispers, she begged me to let her die and join her parents. When our eyes connected, I was astonished to see that they had transformed from violet to a mesmerizing shade of pearl, leaving me speechless.

Her sniffles echoed in the silence as she stared at me, tears welling up and causing her eyes to glisten. "Why are you being so kind to me?" she sobbed, her tear-filled eyes locked onto mine.

"For some reason, I can't help but feel a magnetic pull towards you, Vyolette. And I still care about you... a great deal," I responded earnestly.

She opened her mouth to speak, but the weight of her unspoken words silenced her. I don't know her age or how many years she's spent fending for herself, but one thing I'm certain of is that I'll always be there for her, without question. I need to show her she is not alone in this vast world.

While I let a new bath run for her, I took the first aid kit and tended to her wounds, before washing her and helping her get dressed. I climbed into bed with her, and she laid her head on my chest, mourning quietly as I comforted her. Once she had finally drifted off to sleep, I slipped out of her hold, eager to freshen up and finally rest myself.

With my mind still buzzing from the evening, I retreated to my room and found solace under the cascading water of the shower. Following a refreshing cold shower, I settled onto my bed to watch the news. The screen displayed images of a raging fire, and it was at that moment that Vyolette knocked on my partially open bedroom door. I turned off the television and with an invitation, she stepped inside, her movements deliberate and cautious. I couldn't help but notice her hands fidgeting with the bottom hems of my t-shirt, tugging it slightly over the boxers I had chosen for her to wear.

I hoisted myself up onto the headboard to rest my back against it, my hands gripping the cool metal, and flicked the switch on the lamp, instantly illuminating the room. "Is everything okay, Vyolette?"

In a soft whisper, she questioned, "Can I sleep next to you?" Her words barely reached my ears. "I… I've never slept alone since—"

"Of course you can, sure, come over," I responded before I could think.

Struggling to hold back tears, she managed to give me a soft smile and made her way towards my bed. I gently pulled back the covers, silently inviting her to share the warmth with me. I positioned myself on the bed, and Vyolette snuggled in my arms, her head against my chest once again, and I turned off the lights, allowing the soft glow from the balcony to gently illuminate the room through the thin curtains. As I felt her head shift on me, I glanced down and caught sight of her eyes glowing in the dimly lit room as she looked at me, they were truly mesmerizing.

"Thank you, Axiel," she said once again, before lowering her head and drifting to sleep.

CHAPTER FOUR

YOU THROUGH ME

AXIEL

" Vyolette!"

I swiftly raced towards her, seizing her hand, cradling her limp body in my arms, and sprinting away at an unbelievable speed. With a hurried glance behind, my eyes widened in terror as I saw a nightmarish creature hot on our heels. Instinctively, I looked up and propelled myself into the air, leaping from one tree to another, my heart pounding in my chest as I begged myself to wake up, that this was just a nightmare.

"You're dreaming, Axiel," I cried, my voice filled with urgency. "Wake up! Wake up!"

A sudden force struck me from behind, causing me to lose my balance and crash onto the ground. With Vyolette in my arms, we rolled several times on the uneven ground, each impact jarring my senses, until finally, my back collided forcefully with a protruding rock.

My eyes sprang open, and I was greeted by the gentle warmth of the morning sun filtering through the bedroom window. Sweat trickled down my face as I reached up to touch my head, my fingers coming away moist. Meanwhile, Vyolette remained undisturbed, cradled and sleeping soundly in my arms.

I slid out of bed with caution, making sure not to wake her, and quietly descended the stairs to whip up a delicious breakfast for both of us. I cooked us a simple breakfast comprising a rolled omelet, accompanied by buttered toast and a refreshing side of chopped tomato-spinach salad. While I was blending the banana smoothie to a smooth consistency, my attention was suddenly drawn to Vyolette, who was taking slow, cautionary steps down the stairs, her eyes filled with contemplation.

"Vyolette, are you feeling alright?" I asked, fully aware of what the response would be.

Her gaze met mine, and I found myself drawn into the depths of her mesmerizing eyes, which shimmered with a captivating allure. "So it wasn't just a dream," she stated, her voice hushed and barely discernible. "I—what am I supposed to do now?"

"What do you mean?" I asked

"With my home destroyed, I am left to face a future without my parents, I'm all alone… I… I can't do it," she said with a cracked voice, "I have nowhere else to go, what am I going to do?"

I hurriedly reached for her and wrapped my arms around her, determined to provide comfort. "Vyolette, I want you to know that you're welcome to stay with me for as long as you'd like," I reassured her. "If you're uncomfortable staying with me, I'm sure Monique would be happy to take you in."

She nodded at me, a hint of sadness in her eyes, before shaking her head in disagreement slowly. "Monique may be kind, but her kids are a different story," she confided. "They mock and bully me when she's not around. I don't want to subject myself to that type of treatment, not again."

"Vyolette..."

"I should have been in the house when it burned down!" she said to herself

I guided her to a seat at the table, where the delicious aroma of breakfast wafted through the dining room. I reached out and placed my hand on top of hers, causing her eyes to immediately meet mine in a moment of connection. "Please don't say that," I pleaded, holding her face in my hand, "you're welcome to stay here with me, and there's nobody to insult you or bully you, I promise, I will always protect you."

Her sniffles echoed in my embrace, and she questioned, "Why are you being so nice to me, Axiel?"

"I don't know," I answered truthfully.

She let out a defeated sigh, "I'm sorry but I can't live here with you," she stated, pushing me away and wiping her tears, "I will only be a burden."

"You can't or you don't want to?" I countered

There is a palpable tension in the air as she remains silent, her body trembling with a mix of desire to stay and overwhelming fear. "Would your parents accept me staying here?" she asked breaking the silence

"Honestly, I'm not sure," I replied, scratching my head in uncertainty. "But they're gone for who knows how long, and since I'm eighteen, I don't think they'd mind if I invited a girl to live with me. Especially if she has nowhere else to go... I genuinely believe they won't have an issue with it."

Vyolette sighed, her gaze fixed on the breakfast I had prepared for us. "But if you truly knew me..." she trailed off, leaving her words hanging in the air.

"I'm aware," I responded calmly, not needing any further explanation. "Monique told me everything, and she's right, you are special."

"She didn't tell you everything," Vyolette stated. "She could only tell you what she knew,"

"Then tell me what I need to know," I insisted.

With the smoothies poured and placed on the table, I took a seat beside her, my eyes locked on hers, patiently waiting for her to share her thoughts. Hesitant at first, she eventually found comfort and began sharing the intricate details of her life. Surprisingly, her eyes were not naturally violet, it was only after the accident that they took on that striking hue, whereas they had naturally been a deep shade of gray.

"About nine years ago, my parents and I were heading home from a day at the fair… it was a birthday surprise to me. A driver drove into us, purposely—I know they said it was a drunk driver, but it wasn't—I know I saw him walk over to our overturned car to make sure we were all dead, he checked my parents' pulses, he couldn't reach me so I guess he simply gave up and believed I was dead too."

'*Oh my gawd*,'

"I thought I was dead too but woke up in the hospital, and was told my parents didn't make it," she continued. "While walking with a nurse to the courtyard, I noticed some eerie figures lurking in the shadows, following us. From that moment on, my life was forever changed, as if seeing the first one and acknowledging them was my ultimate downfall. I began seeing more and more souls in the hospital and I felt like I was going crazy."

"Why would someone want to have your family killed?" I asked the more important question.

She shrugged and responded, "I don't know, my parents were normal people, my mother was a maid and my father was a salesman who traveled often."

I didn't inquire any further, instead giving her the time to divulge what she was willing to tell me. Eventually, her grandmother moved her here to Old Matra, providing her with glasses to wear as a precaution whenever she left the house for school—she was made fun of, but nothing out of the ordinary insults of being an orphan by kids in her class. The worst of the bullying began when she was enrolled in Cardale Heights High School. While washing her face, she placed her glasses on the bathroom counter and forgot to take them when she left the washroom.

Walking down the hallway, she was met with a handful of students and teachers who had passed in the halls of the school, she freaked out and had an episode that made her not only the laughingstock but the outcast of the school, that was two years before I was enrolled there.

'If I had enrolled in the first year—' I brushed the thought out of my mind.

"I closed my eyes so hard that day, they bled," she shared, "I just didn't want to see them, I didn't want to see them."

The image of her eyes turning a mesmerizing pearly white in the bathroom kept playing in my mind. Despite my reservations, I knew I had to share this detail with her. "Last night... your eyes, they were as white as pearls," I said, "even the pupils had a creamy shade."

She stared at me confused, "What…? Are you sure it wasn't the lighting?"

"It probably was," I said dismissively.

When she was done opening up to me, I reassured her I still wanted to be by her side and that I saw her as someone unique, not a freak. Similar to how Monique sees her, I also view her as someone special. Despite her internal turmoil, she managed to smile for me again, and we silently ate our breakfast.

While she helped wash the dishes, she expressed her thanks again, her words carrying a deep sense of appreciation and a hint of lingering fear. As our conversation progressed, I shared with her the fact that my parents were absent for most of my teenage life. Nevertheless, I made it clear that their love and concern for me were never in doubt.

"So, you're almost like me then," she frowned, "taking care of yourself?"

"Yeah…"

"The day I woke up and saw my parents cradling me, I was overjoyed," she confessed, "but I later found out that it was only their souls and they showed up because my grandmother had passed away and they didn't want me to be alone,"

After wiping my hand on a kitchen towel, I gently placed my hand on her shoulders. "Well, you're not alone anymore, Vyolette," I stated, "maybe that's why they haven't shown up here, they know you're safe and with me."

With a smile on my lips, I couldn't help but feel a sense of joy as her gaze met mine, the soft gray hue of her eyes shining through her glasses. Her lips parted, on the brink of uttering something, but she ultimately decided to say nothing. Overwhelmed by the intensity of the moment, I hesitantly leaned in, savoring the softness of her lips as our eyes closed in unison.

Before our embrace could deepen any further, the sudden sound of my cell phone ringing shattered the moment. She pulled away, her fingertip touching her now moist lips as her eyes diverted from me.

"I better take this," I said, abruptly excusing myself to the back patio, where a gentle breeze rustled the leaves and the smell of freshly cut grass lingered in the morning air.

ঞ...

"Hello?" I answered

"Good morning, am I speaking with Axiel Knightly?" the person on the other end of the call asked

"Uh, yeah," I answered, "who am I speaking with?"

Before responding, he cleared his throat and introduced himself, "This is Patrick Beau, the fire investigator, I—"

"Yes," I interjected, eager for an update, "what caused the fire? Was it a faulty wire?"

"No, we believe it was arson," he claimed, "could you come down to the Matra police station with Ms. White, we have a few questions to ask her."

"Uh, sure," I answered, "we'll be down there in about ten minutes,"

"Thank you," he replied before cutting off the call.

ॐ...

With a heavy heart and a sense of urgency, I rushed back inside, grappling with the daunting task of informing Vyolette that her home had been intentionally set on fire. For the past two weeks, I've observed her monotonous routine of attending school, keeping to herself—only speaking to me, returning home, going to work, going home again, sleeping, and repeating the cycle. I couldn't comprehend the depths of someone's hatred for her, to the point where they would set her home on fire, thinking she was inside. Could the individuals behind her parents' death be the ones responsible for this as well?

CHAPTER FIVE

SEE THEM

REJANAE

My living room was filled with the laughter and chatter of Britney, Kelly, Cody, Mark, my boyfriend Zac, and I as we debated over what to watch until Kelly's accidental channel change brought us face-to-face with the news with the headline '*Arsonist targets abandoned house, no casualties reported.*'

Kelly exclaimed, "Guys, check it out!" Her eager tone immediately drew the attention of the others.

***

A distressing incident unfolded in Old Matra this morning around 2 am, as an abandoned house was intentionally set on fire, with reports suggesting that a young girl had been living there. Authorities have confirmed that no casualties occurred due to the fire, which is fortunate. The incident has generated concerns among residents and law enforcement personnel.

A blaze ignited the home in the late hours of the night, consuming the abandoned building on 13th Street Matra Drive. Witnesses have provided accounts of flames erupting from the windows of the dwelling, triggering rapid responses from both the fire department and law enforcement. Last night, firefighters engaged in a prolonged struggle against the inferno until they successfully gained control and prevented the flames from extending to adjacent properties, half an hour after 2 am.

Following a thorough investigation, authorities discovered compelling evidence showing that the fire was deliberately started.

"No way," Britney gasped

"Shhhh!" I hissed

"Our initial findings show that this was a case of arson," stated Chief Investigator Patrick Beau, from the Old Matra Police Department. "Thankfully, the young lady who lived in the house wasn't present when the fire happened, and we're doing everything we can to catch the person or persons behind this crazy act," he added.

"As the investigation into the arson attack continues—"

***

Not wanting to hear another word, I seized the remote and abruptly shut off the television. "Hey, we were watching that!" Kelly shouted

I sharply turned my head to the side, shooting her a piercing glare, while Mark quickly pulled her close and offered her solace. "Don't worry babe," he reassured her, "there won't be any evidence linking it back to us."

I couldn't help but roll my eyes at the two of them, but then Zac scoots over to me and envelops me in a warm embrace. "You okay babe," he asked, "I can feel you trembling,"

"I'm fine," I responded, my heart racing in my chest.

"Good," he said sharply, "it was a joke that went a little too far, and since no one saw us, there's no way for anyone to link it back to us."

"If you ask me, it was more like a favor," Britney laughed, "I don't know why you're getting so worked up when it was your idea in the first place, Reja."

"I don't want to spend the rest of my life in prison!" I exclaimed, my voice filled with fear and desperation.

He rolled his eyes and scoffed. "I promise you, as long as we all keep our mouths shut, nobody would know… agreed?"

"Whatever Zac," Britney lashed out

"I thought she was in there," I said to myself, "where would someone like her be at one in the morning?"

"Knowing her, probably a graveyard," Kelly laughed, "Do you think she'll show up at school on Monday?"

"I doubt," I replied, absentmindedly pulling out my phone from my pocket and scrolling through it, "ghost-girl will probably become more unhinged and eventually be confined to an asylum where she rightfully belongs."

"Good riddance, if you ask me,"

"Good riddance," said Mark, "I remember the day I tossed my football at her head in the hallway once, knocked her glasses off, and her eyes became freaky man, she then told me that my ex-girlfriend's ghost was latching onto me. Gave me the freaking creeps, man."

"Wait, you've had an ex-girlfriend?" Kelly asked as her eyebrows furrowed in confusion, "I thought I was your first?"

"No baby, you're the first girl I've ever been in a relationship with," he responded, holding a chin and forcefully planting a soft kiss on her lips, which she willingly accepted.

Knowing he was lying, I rolled my eyes and remembered his previous relationship with a girl who had an unfortunate accident a year before Kelly joined our group. As the news report replayed in my mind, I became restless. Not wanting to stay in the house any longer, I took my father's SUV and drove us all to the shopping mall.

Upon arriving there and parking, we ascended the stairs to the bustling food court on the third floor. We ordered milkshakes with curly fries and settled at a table for six near the barrier, offering a view of the second-floor stores.

As we sat there eating and conversing, Kelly called for our attention. "I say we should—"

"Isn't that ghost girl?" Britney exclaimed, interrupting Kelly mid-sentence, causing Mark to let out a relieved breath.

"Where?" Kelly's eyes darted around everywhere but where Britney pointed.

"Over there!" Britney pushed, "Who's that she's with?"

"Looks like the tall goth dude from physics," said Cody

"Having black hair and a single ear with piercings, a cross earring, and a chain stud doesn't make you a goth Cody," said Kelly

"Wait," Britney gasped, "Reja, isn't that their loser who confessed to you last week?"

"I don't recall," I responded, brushing her off.

Cody explained that, like Vyolette, he fell on the anti-social spectrum. Neither of them knew his name and had only caught glimpses of him at school. Kelly was adamant that he had expressed his feelings for me last week. However, I can't recall it—I rarely acknowledge anyone beneath me. Vyolette made the mistake of crossing my path and humiliating me in gym class last week. That's why I have a target on her—the sound of her name fills me with anger and resentment. She will regret what she did.

"I have an idea," Cody leaned in, a mischievous grin spreading across his face, "what do you say we follow them?"

Kelly laughed excitedly, her mischievous plan forming. "Yeah, we can slip something into their bags and watch as security takes them."

"Genius!" Mark's hand collided with the table in a burst of excitement, creating a resounding bang that startled everyone nearby.

"What do you say babe?" asked Zac, "are you up for it?"

Downing the final bit of my milkshake, I took a moment to study their faces, their beaming expressions reflecting my own intentions. I agreed, and together we left the table. We made our way down the escalator, heading towards the thrift store called ***Second Chance Styles*** they had entered. It didn't surprise me they shopped here—the moment I stepped into the store, a wave of disgust washed over me and I felt dirty just being inside there.

We crouched behind a few clothing racks, observing their movements as they wandered through the store. The guy effortlessly maneuvered a large blue shopping cart ahead of him as Vyolette chose some horrible clothing and put them in the cart.

"Looks like he's taking her shopping," said Britney

"Do you think they're together?" I lowered my voice and posed my question curiously.

"What do you care?" Britney asked in a hard whisper, her eyes narrowing with suspicion.

"Do I look like I give a damn?" I retaliated with a scoff, "I just asked a simple question,"

"So did I," she countered

"Are you sure this isn't too much Axiel?" she asked, "I feel like all these things are costly,"

He laughed at her lightly, "compared to the store I wanted us to go to, the things in here are anything but pricey," he stated, "but we should hurry, we still have a laptop and cellphone to get you,"

"Don't forget groceries," she added

He laughed and pulled her to his side, planting a soft kiss on her head before they continued shopping. Surprisingly, the things they took barely came to pocket change, and we saw nothing in that store worth security getting called on her for.

"We should follow them to the next store," Kelly whispered, her eyes glinting with mischief. "There must be something in there worth the risk of her getting caught."

"Right," Britney nodded in agreement, smiling in a way that freaked even me out.

They walked into an electronics store, and it was exactly what we were looking for. We followed them in at a distance and while Zac and the others kept an eye on them, Britney and I went over to the phone section where she distracted the sales guy so I could get a hold of one of the phones I could put in her side bag.

We got back to the others, the phone in hand and ready for Cody to distract them, when I saw Axiel place a box for a 17-inch laptop, a PS5 game console, and a Samsung Galaxy S22 Ultra on the counter.

"What the fuck!" Kelly gasped

"There's no way they can afford that," I mumbled, "they probably know we're following them and are putting on a show."

"Are you paying by cash, card, or cheque?" the cashier asked

"Card," he answered, fishing his wallet from his back pocket and pulling out a black card I've only seen in some movies.

"It's that a freaking *American Express Centurion Credit Card*?" Kelly took a breath

"What... where?" asked Britney

She pointed at the two, and we watched in hushed anticipation as the cashier swiped the card in the machine, the sound of the magnetic strip gliding against the reader with Axiel entering his pin when requested. Cody and Mark whispered to each other, questioning who he was and speculating on how his family could own such a rare credit card.

"Not even my parents could afford that card!" I hissed, "and we're the richest family in this town next to Zac's,"

I placed the phone I had intended to put in Vyolette's bag on the counter and watched as the two left the store, Axiel, carrying the bags of everything he had bought for her as if they weighed nothing. My friends and I left the store in stunned silence, questioning the logic of putting a $1,200 phone in her bag when Axiel had just purchased one that cost nearly double the price, along with other expensive things for her. It would only make us look stupid if we continued with our plan.

Kelly nudged me playfully, "I betcha regret turning him down now," she laughed

CHAPTER SIX

SEE A NEW LIFE

MAY 13th

VYOLETTE

A month has passed since I started living with Axiel, and today is a bittersweet day for me. It's not only my 18th birthday but also the anniversary of the tragic accident that took my parents away from me. Since then, I've never had a reason to celebrate and therefore, I've never celebrated it again.

The sky was painted with hues of orange and purple as the sun set behind the hills of Old Matra. Axiel is on the couch next to me, him on his phone and me browsing Netflix options for something interesting to watch. What surprises me the most is that he has all these things, but he doesn't dress extravagantly or behave in a snobbish and ignorant manner like most rich people do. Even his car is nothing out of the ordinary.

Startled by his sudden groan, I turned my head to look at him and asked, "What's wrong?"

"I... need a change of scenery," he stated, his voice betraying a touch of restlessness. "It's Saturday night, and I feel like going out to dance would be nice."

A chuckle eluded me as I jokingly nudged him before my expression went serious again. "Not tonight," I said quietly, barely above a whisper.

"Why not?" he asked, concern evident in his tone. "Is something wrong?"

Adjusting my position, I folded my leg beneath me and turned my body towards him. "I wanted to tell you," I began, my voice filled with a mix of vulnerability and pain. "Today is my birthday, but it's also the anniversary of my parents' death. It's hard to find the right way to celebrate it when it feels like I'm also celebrating their death."

"What type of logic is that?" Axiel questioned, commenting whether dwelling on the passing of my parents was what they would want, instead of celebrating the day I entered their lives.

"I know but…"

"When they were with you… their ghosts, what did you do on your birthday?" he asked

"They stopped asking to celebrate it after I refused the first time," I replied, "as much as I wanted to celebrate it with them, it just didn't feel the same,"

Moving closer, Axiel's presence provided me a comforting shield as he held me tightly, offering words of encouragement that I desperately needed. "It's puzzling to me why families, partners, or people in general, opt out of celebrating a birthday or holiday when someone close to them or someone they knew passed away on that day," he began, his tone reflective. "Do you believe your parents would want you to persist in your misery every year on your birthday?" he questioned. "They wouldn't! They wanted you to find joy in the day, even when they couldn't be there physically, they wanted to celebrate it with you."

"I know, but," I hesitated, straining to gather my thoughts for a persuasive argument.

"But nothing," he interjected, "a birthday, holiday, anniversary, whatever special day it is, should always be celebrated, not grieved."

"I… I…"

"Let tonight be your first step, Vyolette," he insisted, "how old are you turning today?"

"Eighteen," I answered

"Perfect," he said excitedly, "there's an 18-30 club nearby. How about we celebrate your birthday there? Are you up for it?"

The last thing I wanted to do, especially tonight, was to be inside a vehicle. I felt a strong sense of hesitation. Despite my reservations, I reluctantly agreed, replying with a half-hearted "Sure..." However, I made a firm decision not to drink any alcohol, as I believed it had the potential to amplify my supernatural powers, even though I had never experienced it.

Together, we climbed the stairs and separated into our respective rooms, each taking the time to get ourselves ready to leave. Half an hour later, I made my way downstairs and found Axiel patiently waiting for me, resting against the back of the couch. I'm standing here, wearing a short, loose black dress that flows with every step I take. I've paired it with a cozy brown jacket and completed the look with black stockings and knee-high boots. Axiel's edgy style was on display as he sported black jeans with knee rips, a white t-shirt featuring a bold black triangle, and a black leather jacket layered over a black hoodie. He topped off the look with a black cap and sleek black and white Nike shoes.

"Wow—oh—wow, Vyolette," he exclaimed, "you look absolutely amazing!" He stumbled over his words, his cheeks turning red in embarrassment.

Grinning, I lightly punched him on his shoulder, enjoying the playful banter between us. "You're not too shabby either," I teased, playfully.

Lost in thought, I felt him move closer and delicately tuck my hair behind my ear. "If only you could take off your glasses for one night," he whispered, "you have such beautiful eyes."

Stuttering nervously, I quickly brushed past him, feeling a rush of anxiety. "T—time to go..."

With a laugh, he trailed behind me to the garage, ensuring that every door was securely locked before we set off. We pulled up to the club after a quick fifteen-minute drive. As we made our way to the entrance, I couldn't help but notice the nervous jitters running through my legs, a feeling I'd never experienced since I'd never been in a place like this.

With a gleeful grin, Axiel embraced me in a side hug and declared, "You're going to have the best birthday ever tonight, an experience that will overshadow the trauma, one you will look back on and be grateful for."

I've lived with Axiel long enough to know that this wasn't his element. We've gone to a few places, like the movies where we shared a tub of buttery popcorn and laughed at the comedy on screen. We've also visited the park, where we strolled hand in hand, enjoying the sound of children's laughter and the scent of freshly cut grass. Another time, we ventured to the amusement park, feeling the thrill of the roller coasters and tasting the sweetness of cotton candy. And there was that memorable day when we went fishing at the lake, feeling the gentle breeze and hearing the calming sound of water lapping against the shore. Last, we even explored a fair once, immersing ourselves in the bright lights, the aroma of fried food, and the excitement of carnival games. The question of why he specifically chose tonight, out of all nights, to go to a club of all places lingered in my mind. Could it be that Monique had informed him about my birthday, and he wanted to do something special for me?

While Axiel engaged in conversation with a formally dressed man in a maroon suit and a white undershirt, I stood near the bar, taking in the buzz of the crowded room. A few minutes later, he returned, and we were led to an exclusive booth in the VIP section of the club, away from the bustling crowd. Axiel ordered two refreshing Virgin Mojitos for us as we settled in our booth.

Despite the privacy of our location, the dance floor remained visible, and the music pounded in our ears, deafeningly loud. Leaning over to me, his lips touching my ear, his warm breath sent a shiver down my spine.

"I understand that today may stir up painful memories, but remember, it's also your special day and you deserve to find joy in it," he gently reminded me.

My drink touched my lips, and as I nodded, I couldn't help but reflect on how he had transformed my life, making it feel whole again. He turned his attention to the dance floor, watching others as they danced, conversed, and moved around—his head bopping to the beat of the song playing. "You wanna dance?" I asked, the music blaring and people twirling around on the dance floor.

With a self-deprecating laugh, he admitted, "I'm a terrible dancer to this type of music,"

"Oh, okay," I muttered, taking another sip of my drink.

"But I'll attempt it just for you," he continued

Downing the last of my drink, I wasted no time in pulling him towards the dance floor. As we set ourselves among the other patrons of the club, the music seamlessly transitioned into a rhythm that made it difficult for me to match my way of dancing. As Axiel and I observed the other dancers, their ungraceful movements filled the air with sensual energy. Suddenly, he discreetly cleared his throat and gently spun me around, pressing my back against his chest. With a firm grip on my waist, he pulled me closer, creating an intimate connection between us. Noting how the other partnered people were dancing, I began seductively sashaying my body, swaying my hips from side to side, moving in a motion that had him doing the same thing behind me.

"I could definitely get used to this," he says with a smile, his hands finding their place on my stomach as we move together, our bodies creating a seamless rhythm.

The world seems to blur as he twirls me around, our eyes locked in a mesmerizing gaze. We move in perfect harmony, and as the music swells, his hips grinding against mine in a sexual motion, he leans in and kisses me, sending an electrifying surge through my body. A moment later, he pulled away, held my chin up, and with his thumb, traced my bottom lip as he bit his slightly. The music takes on a new tone, becoming slow and melodic. "Happy Birthday Vyolette," he whispered, his voice soft and calming while he rested his head gently against mine, his lips parted slightly, making me feel the warmth of his breath against my skin.

His sudden retreat causes a rush of heat to flood my face as if someone had lit a fire beneath my skin. I anxiously nibble on my lower lip. In an instant, he locked lips with me once again, with his other hand, he tenderly caressed my face, his thumb tracing a path along my cheek, intensifying our kiss.

CHAPTER SEVEN

SEE US

REJANAE

School exams are finally over, there's only prom left to attend in the next month, and then graduation. I can't wait to escape from this suffocating prison and breathe in the fresh air of freedom. With my father away on a business trip for the weekend and me not in the mood to go through another house party, my friends and I went down to a popular club, 'Dynesty' in the center of town, to let loose for the evening.

Taking a sip from my martini, I watched Kelly and Mark, along with Cody and Britney, dance with such intimacy that it felt like they thought they were in a private bedroom instead of a crowded club. Zac asked me to dance multiple times, but after a while and him not understanding the word 'NO,' I rejected him with a cutting remark. In frustration, he stormed off and joined two girls on the dance floor. Despite his intentional stare and provocative gestures towards the girl who was dancing in front of him, my attention remained fixed on a matter of utmost importance, rendering his actions irrelevant to me.

Ever since I saw them at the mall, the image of Axiel Knightly has been stuck in my mind. Similar to Vyolette, he was also not active on social media, but I gathered the same amount of information about him as the teachers and principal had—his complete name. He was a complete mystery, normally the principals of schools have all the information about their students, including their full name, date of birth, parents' names, and even their medical history, but the only thing Mr. Jakins knows about him is his full name, he doesn't even have his parents name far less their occupation, pressing him for answers with threats did no progress, so it's all a complete mystery.

Whenever I encountered him at school, he seemed inseparable from that eerie ghost girl. They arrived and left together as if they were living in the same house, I don't even know where he lives to say I can go to his place and talk to him. One day, while my friends were at practice, curiosity got the better of me, so I followed them home. However, after going through a winding path in the woods he drove into, I somehow ended up right back at the entrance, which left me bewildered. Regardless of my attempts, the outcome remained unchanged, even when I made the effort on foot.

My friends returned, visibly exhausted, and collapsed onto the seat next to me. Britney's eyes widened in surprise as she lifted her drink to her lips. "Oh... My... Gosh!" she gasped, "Look who just walked through the door!"

Amused, Cody questioned with a playful grin on his face. "Is that ghost girl?"

"No way!" Mark's voice caught in his throat as he struggled to find the right words, finally saying, "She looks... HOT!"

"Excuse me?" Kelly snapped at him, "I dare you to say that again!"

Clearing his throat, Mark reached over and snatched Kelly's drink, quickly gulping it down. Watching her at the bar, I couldn't deny the captivating presence she exuded, just as Mark had pointed out. Despite her glasses, she looked stunning, even better than me, I dare say. I loathed it.

I made a notion that we should humiliate her, and what better way to do that than to slip her a fun pill and send a few strangers her way? She had no right to be in a place like this and should stick to her rundown shed.

I took the packet Zac always had on hand and held it between my fingers. "So… who's gonna give it to her?"

"I'll do it," Mark declared confidently, his finger flicking the packet with anticipation, eager to see the outcome.

With a swift motion, Cody extended his arm and pointed in her direction. "Wait, who's that with her?"

As we glanced over, a tall, impeccably dressed man caught our attention. His cool demeanor was captivating as he walked up to her, confidently wrapping his arm around her waist and gesturing toward the club's manager. My eyes widened in astonishment as I saw them being escorted to the VIP lounge, a section reserved solely for the elite few who possessed immense wealth.

I squinted my eyes, getting a clearer view of his face amidst the dim lighting of the club. "But who's that with her?" I questioned, as though Cody hadn't asked the same question only seconds ago.

"No clue..." said Britney, "It's hard to tell in this lighting."

"Guys, I think it's that Axiel dude she was at the mall with," said Zac

At that moment, it all clicked—Axiel, his face, his name, everything came rushing back. A week after the fire at Vyolette's place, I vividly remember a tall, nerdy-looking emo guy with a deep voice confessing his love to me. I didn't hesitate to turn him down and, in no uncertain terms, told him to fuck off. The reason? His unsettling appearance encompassed a black knitted sweater over an undershirt, paired with black jeans that didn't look like they cost over twenty dollars. The sight of him disgusted me, as his apparent poverty was clear, and he couldn't even manage to tip my maids. Looking at him treat the freak made me somewhat jealous, why am I feeling so jealous?

"Damn, he looks fucking hot without his glasses," Kelly voiced, eying him like he was a meal.

"Ahem!" With irritation, Mark cleared his throat, trying to regain his composure.

Britney laughed and nudged me, "You called him a loser, a geek, and then you poured your smoothie all over his head before telling him to fuck off," she taunted, "still think that way?"

"You're definitely regretting it," Kelly added

"Why would she give a fuck?" Zac lashed out, "I'm her fucking boyfriend and I look better, more buff than that little fucktard!"

I scoffed, rolling my eyes in exasperation before reluctantly agreeing with Zac. A while later, they went back to enjoy themselves, and I watched unimpressed and unfazed as Zac swapped spit with the two girls he had been dancing with earlier.

While searching for Axiel, I witnessed him being forcefully dragged onto the dance floor by the freak, causing my anger to escalate like a boiling kettle. I walked over to a corner and positioned myself to have a full view of them. Mesmerized by their intimate dance, I found myself unconsciously caressing my body, imagining that it was his touch I was feeling and when he turned her to face him, a surge of jealousy overwhelmed me, especially when I witnessed him passionately kissing her. I felt a sinking sensation in my chest, desperately wishing that I was the one he was kissing and bringing back home with him.

'I'm right over here... why can't you see me?' I pondered silently, questioning my thoughts.

"Reja, what are you doing?" Britney asked, forcefully shoving me, which made me stumble before regaining my balance.

"What the hell, Brit!" I screamed, my voice filled with anger.

I quickly averted my gaze, hoping she wouldn't notice, but it was already too late since she knew exactly who I was keeping an eye on. With a sly grin, she looks at me and raises an eyebrow. "So, you've got a thing for the loser, huh?" she claimed, "I wonder what Zac's gonna say about this,"

"I don't know what you're talking about," I replied, rolling my eyes in exasperation.

"You never do, sweetie," she said in a singsong voice. "If it makes you feel any better, I found out that they're just friends, but she actually lives with him."

I rolled my eyes so hard they pained me, already aware that they lived together. "They look like more than friends to me!" I replied, "Besides, it doesn't matter, I'm with Zac."

"I don't give a damn!" she shouted, her words dripping with contempt. "All I want is for you to snatch that card he's wasting, using on that freak."

"I'm many things, but I'm not a thief Brit," I retaliated

"UGH, come on Reja," she groaned, "that creep has been following you around school since day one, I'm sure he will give it to you if you simply bat your eyelashes and ask."

I agreed to do it, not because I agreed with her, but because I wanted a reason to speak to him. Holding my drink, I made my way towards them and tapped Axiel on the shoulder, who was engrossed in a too-passionate kiss with Vyolette.

"Can I cut in?" I ask directly, leaving no room for ambiguity.

He abruptly stopped kissing Vyolette, and his attention shifted to me, his eyes narrowing with suspicion. "Rejanae…, y—you're speaking to me...?"

"Is that a problem?" I asked, casually flipping my hair over my shoulder.

"Uhhh..." he stuttered

"Wanna buy me a drink?" I asked, playfully batting my eyelashes, hoping he could see them through the soft rave lighting.

He tilted his head to the side, his fingers tightening around Vyolette's hand. "You have a drink in your hand," he responded, gesturing towards the untouched drink I held.

With a mischievous grin, I playfully laughed and splashed my drink onto Vyolette's chest before nonchalantly tossing the glass behind me. "What drink?"

With a deep, guttural growl, she bared her teeth, emanating a fierce and primal energy as she glared at me. "What the hell!" she snapped, "you did that on purpose!"

"Go clean yourself up," I commanded, my voice firm and authoritative. "I need to speak to Axiel alone—I looked her up and down—without any unwanted interruptions."

When I saw she was about to cry, a smirk formed on my lips. Axiel quickly reached out and grabbed her hand, preventing her from running away. With a firm grip, he pulled her towards him, his hand finding its place on her back, providing the support she needed. A flicker of contempt crossed my face as I observed this, causing the corner of my lips to twitch uncontrolled yet slowly.

"She's not going anywhere," he said through gritted teeth.

"Is she the reason you don't want to be with me?" I snapped, raising my voice, ready to humiliate him for taking her side—for choosing her over me.

He raised his eyebrows in surprise at my comment. "If I recall correctly, the last time we spoke—when I confessed my lust for you, you told me to fuck off and never bother you again before drenching me," he retaliated, "who the fuck are you to tell my girl to leave?"

"Your girl?" I scoffed, surprised, taking a small step back, "Are you seriously with this freak?"

His eyes darkened, and he spoke through gritted teeth, "Say what you want about me but insult Vyolette again, and I swear I will make you regret it!"

Out of nowhere, Zac stormed over and forcefully pushed Axiel, calling Vyolette a freak and a bitch before warning him he would beat him up for daring to talk to me. In one fluid motion, Axiel seized him by the throat, hoisting him into the air, and then effortlessly flinging him aside. My body was paralyzed with astonishment, rendering me speechless and motionless.

Abruptly, the music ceased, and a hushed silence fell over the club as the crowd gathered around us. Rushing to Zac's aid, Cody and Mark swiftly assisted him in regaining his footing. Kelly and Britney came to my side, their voices filled with anger as they unleashed a barrage of curses and insults toward Axiel for choosing Vyolette over me.

"You're pathetic," Britney snapped, "Just last week you told her you love her and want to be with her, and now you're with the freak of the town!"

Axiel's eyes grew even darker, a flicker of dark violet appearing in them as he warned, "Do not test my patience."

As he walked away with Vyolette on his arm, I hastily clung onto Britney and Kelly's arms, desperately trying to keep them from pursuing him. I couldn't shake off the eerie feeling that there was more to him than met the eye—his eyes, the look in his eyes—something about him simply wasn't human.

"You're just gonna let them walk away after what he did to Zac?" Kelly barked

I shook my head vigorously, vehemently rejecting the reality of what had just unfolded. “No… I’m not!”

CHAPTER EIGHT

SEE DECISIONS

AXIEL

Before, I always imagined when Rejanae would approach me and start a conversation. Unfortunately, the way she approached Vyolette and me tonight and spoke to us made me feel an intense desire to punch her in the face. The memory of lifting Zac and effortlessly tossing him across the dance floor came rushing back, I know I'm strong, but I was not that strong to do so without breaking a sweat.

It was a quiet drive back to my place, the only sound being the hum of the engine and the tires against the road. I despised the fact that tonight was meant to be a great and memorable, filled with joyous occurrences and memories to counteract the painful memory of Vyolette's parents' passing, but it was completely shattered by Rejanae and her entourage. I stole a glance at Vyolette and noticed her deep in contemplation, her hand lightly resting on her damp chest as she peered through the window.

"Vyolette, are you okay?" I asked with a sense of worry in my voice.

"Yeah, I'm fine," she replied, her wistful gaze fixed on the moonlit night outside, her hand gently resting on the window seal.

"Hey," I reached over and gave her hand a gentle squeeze, suggesting, "Let's keep the night going, Vy. When we get home, we can make some popcorn, find a movie to watch, or even have a fun dance party together."

"Axiel…"

"I promised to make this day unforgettable for you, Vyolette," I reminded her, intertwining her fingers with mine before bringing her hand to my lips and gently pressing them against the back of her hand. "And I meant it."

Approaching the stop sign, I slowed my car to a halt, leaned over, and gave her a tender kiss on her cheek. Meeting her has brought me immense joy, and a sense of completion to my life—I didn't know a part of me was missing until we locked lips tonight. Her company is everything I could have wished for and more.

Scanning the road for any approaching vehicles, I was taken aback when a car unexpectedly sped up from behind and forcefully crashed into the back of my car, propelling it to the center of the road, right in the path of an oncoming truck.

"AXIEL!"

In a split second, I shouted, "VYOLETTE!" and instinctively shielded her, the seatbelt giving way under my force.

HALF AN HOUR PRIOR
REJANAE

The way that nerd spoke to me, acting as if he were above me and embarrassing me in front of everyone, was utterly infuriating, and I refused to let him go unpunished. There was no denying his wealth and affluent origins and I am at the point where I could not care less about the intrigue surrounding him—if I can't have him, then I refuse to let that freak have him either. Cody quickly settled our bill, and we hastily departed the club, wanting to avoid the continuing humiliation of being laughed at by the crowd.

"What the hell happened back there?" Zac coughed as he entered the passenger seat of Britney's father's SUV, "That skinny dude had the strength of Superman—what the fuck!"

With the door still ajar, I swiftly maneuvered out of the parking lot, feeling the adrenaline rush through my veins like a surge of electricity. Turning the corner abruptly, the force sent my friends tumbling to the opposite side of the jeep, while Kelly fumbled to buckle her seatbelt.

"What the fuck Reja, where's the fire?" Britney barked.

"Reja, can you slow the fuck down," Mark pleaded, "you're gonna hit someone."

Desperate to catch up with them before they disappeared into the woods, I ignored the stop signs and sped up the vehicle, my heart pounding, until I caught a glimpse of his cheap SUV waiting at a stop sign. I stopped abruptly, aligning my jeep precisely with the back of Axiel's SUV, revving the engine as I glared at its rear.

Leaning forward from the back seat, Kelly questioned me with a firm grip on my seat. "Reja, what are you doing?"

"What does it look like?" I responded through gritted teeth, "I need to teach those losers a lesson!"

As the jeep idled for a moment, Zac leaned in, his voice filled with concern, "What's your plan, babe?" he asked as I pressed on the gas again, determined.

"What does it look like?" I retaliated.

"Something stupid!" Mark cried, quickly fastening his seatbelt.

"No way!" cried Britney "I can't get another dent in my car, my dad will think I was driving drunk again!"

"I know someone who could fix it, so don't worry about it!" I responded.

"Reja, don't do this!" Kelly begged, "Burning down her home was easy, but causing an accident, that's going too far, even for you, Reja!"

"I'm not gonna hurt them," I lied, my voice laced with false reassurance. "I'm only gonna scare them! If you don't wanna stay, then leave!"

Her voice rose in protest as she declared, "I'm out of here! I refuse to be a part of your jealous revenge."

"Fine by me!" I replied, my fingers gripping the steering wheel tighter.

They all climbed out of the jeep and slammed the doors shut behind them, their voices dissipating into the distance, leaving me alone with my decision. With a deep breath, I shifted gears and floored the pedal, the engine roaring to life as I raced towards their jeep, determined not to let them escape. The jeep violently crashed into the back of Axiel's SUV, propelling them into the path of an approaching 18-wheeler truck. I slammed on the brakes and stopped with a screeching halt, just in time to prevent any major harm to Britney's father's jeep, although the front bumper suffered significant damage from the collision. Thankfully, my father's mechanic would be able to repair it without a problem.

The sight of the truck crushing Axiel's SUV, dragging it a good distance and through a barrier, brought a gratifying smirk to my face. Satisfied with my accomplishment, I drove back to the others where Britney was standing on a rock with her hand outstretched, desperately searching for a signal on her phone while Mark comforted Kelly as she cried in his arms.

Barking fiercely, I honked my horn, the sharp sound piercing through the dead silence of the deserted road and catching their attention. "Will you fucktards hurry up and get in?"

"What the fuck did you do Rejanae," Britney cried, tears streaming down her face as she entered the car.

"They're dead, they're dead," she cried, "we're going to jail 'cause they're dead!"

As I drove off, Zac and Cody glanced back at the wreckage, their faces filled with shock and concern. Despite Mark's suggestion to call '911', I dismissed it and stubbornly declined. The sound of Britney's desperate cries for not wanting to go to jail pierced through the loud rampage inside the jeep, igniting a powerful urge within me to toss her off a cliff. She's acting like we haven't done worst things before.

With the fear of being put behind bars gripping him, since this, what I did was act without a plan, Cody cried, his voice filled with terror. "What have you done Reja!" he questioned, "If they die, we could go to prison."

"Relax dumbass!" I responded, annoyed. "My uncle is a cop and my grandfather is a judge, they'll never let that happen. Let's just do what we usually do and pretend as if we were never there!"

VYOLETTE

'Vyolette… Vyolette can you hear me?' a faded voice with familiarity called, 'I'm so sorry Vyolette, we tried so hard to shield you from this.'

'We're so sorry Vy,' another familiar voice apologized

My gaze swept across the surroundings and settled on a picturesque, white wooded area that unfolded before me. Peering through the trees, I spotted two majestic figures standing tall, illuminated by a brilliant white light.

'Mom…, Dad…?' I called

As I fought to make my way toward the vanishing figures, an eerie, guttural growl echoed through the surroundings. Frantically scanning my surroundings, my eyes finally settled on a mysterious, shadowy figure. The sight of its menacing, sharp teeth sent a shiver down my spine, causing my heart to momentarily stop.

'So… you've awakened,' an unknown dark menacing voice stated, 'don't worry, I'll find—'

The repeated beeping noises echoed in my ear, pulling me out of my dreamlike trance, and becoming a haunting reminder of the place I found myself in. I knew all too well the dread that awaited me there. With my eyes still closed, I carefully swept my hands across my body, checking for any signs of injury or discomfort. Besides the IVs in my hand, everything else seemed to be okay.

'Oh, no! I'm at a hospital!'

I have not been to a hospital since I woke up from a coma after my accident about a decade ago, and that was one of the worst days of my life. I knew if I opened my eyes now, there would be countless lost souls after me, begging me to help them. Panic flooded me as I frantically searched for my glasses, knocking over what was not. With uncertainty, I reached out my hand towards what I believed was the end table, hoping to confirm my glasses' presence through touch.

"You're awake," said a nurse

Still searching blindly, I questioned aloud, my voice echoing through the room. "Where are my glasses?"

"Miss, can you open your eyes?" he asked, "you just had a bad car accident and I need to check them,"

"No," I covered my eyes with both my hands, "I'm fine, I don't want you checking my eyes,"

"Miss, please," he pressed, "you don't have a choice—"

"I said I don't want to check them!" I shouted, the sound of my outburst reverberating through the room and causing a few things to shatter.

Despite his best efforts, I refused to open my eyes. Slightly freaked out at what had just happened, he reluctantly handed me my glasses, and I nervously slid them onto my face. Seeking answers, I asked the nurse what happened and how I had gotten here, my memory was foggy, with only a recollection of leaving the club with Axiel before everything became a blur. He shared the limited information he had with me, I was in a horrific accident, and both the emergency response team and first responders were astounded to see us outside of the mangled jeep. They were relieved to find us safe, considering the condition of the vehicle.

As soon as he was done telling me what happened, the doctor came in and saw the state of the room, "what happened here?" he questioned

The nurse shrugged his shoulders, a puzzled expression on his face, and admitted, "I have no clue."

With a determined stride, the doctor approached me and began assessing my vitals. "Hello, my name is Dr. Gumn, how are you feeling?" he asked, his tone professional yet compassionate

"Where's Axiel?" With concern in my voice, I asked, "Is he okay?"

"The young man that was in the accident with you?" he questioned

"Yeah…"

"He's in a coma," he replied, "considering the scene I was described, I'm surprised to see how few injuries the two of you walked away with," he said, his voice filled with disbelief.

"A coma?" I ignored him, "is he gonna be okay?"

"Yes, just a minor head injury, so he's gonna be fine," he replied, "he's doing remarkably well, but we don't expect him to wake up anytime soon, there's little to no brain activity on his end."

The weight of his words pressed down on me as if an invisible force were crushing my spirit. I struggled to accept their veracity, sensing a dishonest undertone in his every utterance. His words faded into background noise as I recalled Axiel's promise—I refused to believe the doctor's words, Axiel promised he would never leave my side, and that was a promise I believed he would keep.

"Could I see him?" I asked

"I'm sorry, miss, but you won't be able to walk for a few weeks and we're still waiting on the new set of wheelchairs," Dr. Gumn voiced, "I said you came out of the accident with minor injuries, but I never said unscathed."

"What are you talking about?" I questioned, "I'm fine, I feel fine,"

His hand outstretched, the nurse promptly handed him a sizeable brown envelope. He took it from her, opened it, and showed me an X-ray of my legs, both were broken. I stared at him confused, I moved my legs and I could feel them moving beneath me. Not wanting to bring attention to myself, I said nothing.

"Get some rest, Ms. White," Dr. Gumn instructed, "we'll let you know as soon as Mr. Knightly wakes up.

I watched their retreating figures, the sound of their footsteps fading away before I finally found solace by resting my head against my pillow. For a fleeting moment, I closed my eyes tightly, desperately hoping and praying for Axiel to be okay, and wake up.

➔A WEEK LATER

It had been an arduous week, but the thought of finally departing from the hospital brought me immense joy. My recurring nightmare kept haunting me as I anxiously paced about, and when the nurse walked in and saw me doing so, it was obvious that my legs were not broken. He called the doctor, who shared his flabbergasted reaction and suggested running some tests on me, but I vehemently declined. Now that I was no longer a minor and was eighteen, I asserted my rights, clarifying that I couldn't be coerced into doing anything or having anything I didn't want being done to or on me. This caused them to back down.

After getting dressed and collecting the belongings they had brought back from the wreckage, I had to go check on Axiel. When I turned around to leave, I saw him walking towards me, his expression filled with relief, I was too relieved to realize he had opened and closed the door without making a sound.

"Oh my gosh Axiel, you're okay," I cried, rushing to him and throwing myself into his embrace.

He wrapped his arms around me tightly, showering my neck with gentle kisses, taking a deep breath, and drawing me closer as if savoring my fragrance as his embrace grew even tighter. "Vyolette…"

"I thought I'd lost you!" we said in sync, our words flowing seamlessly together.

As we both laughed, he gently lowered his head and kissed me, his smile lingering as our heads leaned against each other. Out of the corner of my eye, I caught a glimpse of some nurses peering at us curiously through the window of the room facing the hall.

"The doctor said you were in a coma," I voiced, "I was about to come see you,"

"I'm here now," he replied confidently, his words echoing with a sense of permanence.

With tears streaming down my face, I lifted my glasses to wipe them away, only to be startled by the sight of shadowy figures in the distance. Axiel saw my discomfort and his grip tightened around me as he whispered, "Let's go home."

"Please let's..." I agreed

Exiting the hospital, we were met with lingering gazes from the staff. He instinctively drew me nearer, his smile radiating warmth as our eyes locked. "Don't pay attention to them," he whispered

"Is it okay to let her leave?" A nurse softly whispered as we walked past.

CHAPTER NINE

SEE US LEAVE

AXIEL

When Vyolette and I arrived home three days ago, I found myself tossing and turning all night long, and I had yet to fall asleep. My mind had been wandering a lot since I left the hospital and as distant as my home was away from the town, I wanted to go further. Now that the senior exams were finished, the school was only open to those students who had to rewrite their exams and participate in additional classes. As far as I knew, no other students were allowed to enter the school grounds until prom, and the last thing I wanted to do right now was to stay here in this house, in this town—with Vyolette.

"Morning Axiel," she greeted as she stepped into the kitchen.

"Morning, Vyolette," I responded with a burst of excitement in my voice.

A groan eluded her lips, filled with exhaustion. "Why are you so happy this morning?"

My response came swiftly, filled with enthusiasm. "Why are you so grumpy?"

With a shift in her gaze, she made her way towards me and gently embraced me. "I had a bad dream again," she murmured, before settling down on the barstool next to me.

"Really… what was it about?" I asked inquisitively, wanting to know more.

"That's the thing," she replied, "I can barely recall the details. It's like there's a heavy weight on my head every time I attempt to remember. Sometimes, when I look around, all I see are the white, barren woods. Other times, I feel a creeping darkness, as if it's trying to consume me every time I fall asleep. It's terrifying, Axiel. I'm scared, and I don't know what to do."

Her tear-stained face was buried in my chest, I held her close, murmuring words of comfort and support. She was going through so much and I believed the accident we went through only made things worse for her mental state. "What do you think of the idea of getting away for a bit?" I suggested.

Her tear-filled gray eyes glistened behind her glasses as she looked up at me. "Where will we go?"

"Somewhere far from here," I responded, "but it's only for a while…"

"How long is a while?" she questioned, "are we gonna miss graduation?"

Her question instantly transported me back to the first week she spent here. While comforting her, she sobbed uncontrollably, heartbroken over the realization that her parents would never witness her graduation as they had promised. As the night went on that night, I comforted her with the assurance that, although they remained unseen, she could trust that they were there, watching her walk across that stage and accepting her diploma, and the same thing would happen if she chose to go to college. "No," I answered, "we'll only be away for a week, we'll be back in time for the prom and graduation isn't until the week after."

Initially, she hesitated, concerned about the possibility of getting hurt again by leaving the house. However, I reassured her it was not a risk. In a terse conversation, I informed her about a lake house tucked away in a secluded area in the woods, a three-hour drive from here we could go to and spend a week in solace. It would be our private oasis, free from any disturbances, where we could enjoy a peaceful week.

"You have a lake house?" She questioned, "Like your very own house? That you own?"

"Is that so hard to believe?" I asked

As she wiped her tears and let out a forced laugh, she slowly glanced around my home before refocusing her gaze on me. "I guess not," she said, her tone filled with a mix of realization and understanding, "I just keep forgetting that you're anything but average in terms of your finances."

"I don't let my parents' financial situation affect my mindset," I replied, rubbing her arms as I looked into her eyes. "I'm different from those typical arrogant rich kids who belittle others because of money, and I don't think anyone knows how rich my family is considering my parents act and dress like they're in the lower-middle class."

"I've known that for a while now," she says, her warm smile reaching her eyes. "About you I mean…"

→→→

The sound of sizzling bacon filled the kitchen as I watched her attentively as she made breakfast, my thoughts wandering aimlessly. When she finished making breakfast and sat down to eat, she asked how we would get to the lake house, considering my SUV was completely wrecked and in the junkyard.

I let her know that we had the option to use my mother's *Toyota RAV4 HYBRID*, which was conveniently parked in the second garage on the far side of the house. This was a place I had not shown her, and she hadn't explored it on her own.

After our meal, we made our way back to our rooms to pack up. As Vyolette took a quick break in the washroom, I took the opportunity to bring the suitcases down to the car, waiting for her patiently inside it for us to leave.

VYOLETTE

I finished braiding my hair and then secured it with a ponytail to make sure it wouldn't come undone. As I looked at my reflection in the mirror, my mind wandered slightly, Axiel was taking me away for a week, away from this town and I felt like we should have done so for my birthday instead of now. If we had gone there instead, I wouldn't be having these recurring nightmares—I could really use this vacation.

Before making my way downstairs, I went back to my nightstand to retrieve the small box that had miraculously survived the fire, its contents holding immeasurable sentimental value. I found it perplexing that the necklace and its box somehow managed to survive the fire, while everything else was reduced to ashes.

On my sixteenth birthday, my father told me about a necklace and showed me its exact location. When I found it, he told me to promise him I wouldn't wear it until I turned eighteen, a promise I had faithfully kept and thought I would break after the chaos of the night my home was engulfed in flames—I thought it was lost.

I hear a soft knock on the door panel and turn to see Axiel standing in the doorway. "Ready to go?" he asks, his voice filled with anticipation. I turned to face him fully and his eyes were drawn to the pendant on my chest, "is that from your dad?" he questioned.

'*How could he possibly be aware of something I never disclosed to him?*' I questioned in thought, "What did you just say?" I pressed.

"I asked if you're ready to go?" he repeated, "We still have to stop at the supermarket to buy groceries to cook for the week and there's a long drive ahead of us."

"Oh… okay," I said, holding my head and contemplating if I had misheard him, "I'll be right down,"

"Okay," he said as he turned around, "I already set the alarm, so I'll wait for you in the car."

His departure left me standing there, puzzled, his comment lingering in my thoughts. I'm truly grateful for everything he's done for me, for opening his home to me when he did. From the moment our lips met that evening of my birthday, I've perceived Axiel in a whole new way, and I can't deny that I'm developing feelings for him. After leaving the bathroom, I descended the stairs and was greeted by the sight of the car parked outside, engine purring. Our bags were already placed inside on the back seats, and Axiel was in the passenger seat, ready for our journey.

"What are you doing, Axiel?" I asked, confused, "Are you not driving?"

"I think you should drive," he insisted, "you got your license two weeks ago and it should be time you put it to use,"

"What's going on with you, Axiel?" I asked, puzzled by his odd behavior. "Are you feeling okay?"

"I'm feeling fine," he replied with a sly smile, "Just trying to break you out of your comfort zone."

"If you say so," I replied, walking over to the driver's side and getting in.

With him guiding me, I pulled out of the driveway and headed towards the nearest supermarket, which was just a ten-minute drive away. As I slowed down at a stop sign, an uneasy feeling washed over me. I would not call it a phobia, but as the car came to a halt, my eyes darted in every direction.

"Is something wrong?" Axiel questioned.

Wearily, I let out a sigh, "I am not a fan of stop signs," I voiced.

With a forced chuckle, he looked at me and spoke, his voice carrying a tone of both sympathy and urgency. "I don't blame you, Vy," he said, his eyes filled with empathy, his hand resting on mine, giving it a gentle, reassuring squeeze. "But you mustn't allow the fear of the past to overshadow your resolve to continue moving ahead toward a better future."

With a grateful smile and a tender kiss on his cheek, I redirected my attention back to the road ahead. En route to the back to the lake house, we made a brief pit stop at the nearest supermarket, a one-story grocery store conveniently located just a short stroll away from a gas station. As we pushed the cart through the aisles of the store, I glimpsed Axiel adding some strangely familiar ingredients to our cart.

"Axiel, do you have something planned for dinner?" I asked cautiously, "You're putting quite some ingredients in here..."

"Long week," he chuckled, rubbing his stomach. "I'm ravenous, so I'm looking forward to devouring a generous amount of food tonight and throughout the week."

"You've been eating like a pig for the last three days," I remarked as I observed his slender figure, "I'm surprised you haven't gained any weight."

"Really?" he laughed, "I feel like I haven't eaten in ages. I best go get another cart then."

I pulled him back to me and said it was fine, the cart we had was pretty big and could hold more than we would need for the week, he agreed but left me for a while to grab some more things. Gathering more groceries and toiletries, and putting them in the cart, I handpicked items I believed would be necessary for our stay at the lake house. When I turned the corner and made my way down the meat aisle, an eerie sensation suddenly crawled up my spine as if someone were silently observing our every move.

CHAPTER TEN

SEE ISOLATION

REJANAE

My father has spent the last four hours hurling insults at me, his voice filled with frustration and regret, but I remain indifferent to his hurtful words. I don't know who told him, but somehow he found out what I did to Vyolette and Axiel. He stormed back from his business trip this morning, ready to unleash his anger on me.

"What the fuck were you thinking Rejanae, are you insane!" my father exploded, "you caused them to run off the fucking road?"

"Will you relax, daddy," I scoffed, "they survived, didn't they? It's not like they saw me anyway," I flicked my nail and rolled my eyes, crossing my leg unbothered.

He walked over to the wall and delivered a forceful blow, causing a hole to form. Our home was constructed from solid concrete—not drywall. I've made my father upset before, but not upset enough for him to be physical. With trembling words, I confessed my fear to him, and his piercing glare only heightened my unease. If looks had lethal power, I'd be annihilated.

"Rejanae," he questioned angrily, rubbing his thumb over his knuckles, "do you have any idea whose son was in that accident you stupidly caused?"

Crossing my legs the other way, I leaned my back against the sofa and scoffed, dismissively waving him off. "Some loser nerd and his bitch of a freak who screams about ghosts," I replied nonchalantly.

My father let out a weary sigh, his fingers absentmindedly combing through his golden locks. "I can't do this anymore," he said, frustrated, as he removed his jacket. "You're not a child anymore, Rejanae. You're not in middle school, and I'm tired of covering up your mistakes—this, what you did—that is something I cannot and will not even attempt to cover up."

"Daddy, what are you talking about?" I asked, puzzled.

"You're going to be eighteen the night after your prom, and as soon as you do, I want you out of this house," he stated, "I'm no longer funding your lifestyle and will no longer be covering your mistakes,"

"W—what are you saying, daddy?" I cried, sitting upright, "Are… are you… are you—"

"I'm cutting you off, Rejanae!" he barked

"Daddy, no, please," I begged, "you can't do that!"

"I just did," he said through gritted teeth, "and stay the fuck away from those two!" he added, storming out of the room and leaving the house.

As I heard his hammer rumble out of the yard, the sound of the engine slowly diminishing, a wave of anger washed over me. My father had never displayed such anger before, not even when he learned I knew my mother was cheating on him and even helped her cheat.

I quickly grabbed my keys and headed out to pick up my friends. Together, we planned to visit the convenient store, purchase some alcoholic drinks, and then make our way to the cliff. While walking down the beverage aisle, our baskets filled to the brim with the strongest of what was on the shelves along with a litter of coke to chase it down, Mark caught sight of Vyolette pushing a cart filled with groceries, gliding down the empty aisle, and pointing her out to us.

"I guess that club night was a one-night look only," Britney joked,

When I saw her dressed in the black and white knee-length sundress and black knitted sweater, with black boots, her hair combed in its usual side-over-the-shoulder ponytail, I scoffed. "Looking like a freak, as always, I see."

"Surprised the bastard's not with her," Zac questioned, "thought they were joined at the hip,"

"Dunno," I folded my arms, "maybe he finally came to his senses,"

"Last I heard, he was in a coma," Kelly voiced, "For some reason, even my dad couldn't get more information out of the doctors who were called in to care for them and he's the CEO of the hospital."

"There's a total mystery around Axiel and his family," I voiced, "as much as I want to go over there and knock her the fuck out, my father told me to stay away from them—I… let's go."

They all agreed, and we made our way to the cashier to pay for our drinks. I didn't care what my father said about him and that bitch, she was going to pay for humiliating me, I will make sure she knows her place and crawl back into the grave she came out of.

'Your last day will be your worst day!' I said through gritted teeth, turning on my heel and following my friends to the cashier.

VYOLETTE

The drive up to Axiel's lake house was buzzing with lively conversation and laughter from us, playing games to pass the time. The long drive had left me exhausted, so Axiel decided to take short breaks at various scenic spots to rejuvenate ourselves and take in the views. Unfortunately, we couldn't stay for long, as Axiel was concerned about reaching our destination before nightfall.

Following his instructions, I maneuvered through a corridor of slender trees, their branches brushing against the sides of the car. As I emerged from the tunnel-like terrain, a picturesque lake house materialized in the distance before me, nestled beside a serene lake, with the sun casting its final golden rays on the horizon and the first quarter moon was already making its appearance above the lake, illuminating the surroundings with its ethereal light.

"Wow," I gasped, bringing the car to a stop near the log lake house, mesmerized by the breathtaking view. "Axiel, this place is beautiful!"

"Thought you might like it," he replied, "and I'm sure the dawn is just as gorgeous as the sunset, and we can lounge on the deck and watch the moon and stars when the moon is full."

Overwhelmed with excitement, I embraced him tightly and expressed my gratitude for bringing me to this serene place where I had never experienced such inner tranquility. "I want to make the best of this place... with you, Axiel," I voiced

Axiel interlaced his fingers with mine, and I felt a warmth spread through my hand. Eliminating every space between us, he kissed me deeply, his arms wrapping around me tighter. We break apart at last, and in that fleeting moment, our eyes meet in an endless, profound exchange. Upon noticing a sudden change in his eyes, I inquired if something was amiss, but he adamantly denied it.

"Are you sure?" I pushed

He sighed lightly and turned his gaze to the view in the distance, "I… I want you to see me, Vyolette," he said, his tone weary.

"What do you mean?" I replied, "See you? See you, Axiel? I'm confused. I can see you perfectly,"

With a slight shake of his head and a swallow, he mustered up the courage to say, "You don't truly see me, Vyolette."

"But I do see you," I replied, my confusion evident in my voice. "I can see you standing right in front of me."

His hesitant movements gave away his uncertainty as he reached for my glasses, but I reacted instinctively, tightly holding onto them and begging him not to take them off. “It’s okay,” he said, his voice soft. “Please… open your eyes,”

“What if there were people who died here?” I cried, “We’re in the woods, who knows how many shallow—”

“Vyolette, it’s just you and me here,” he interrupted, his voice filled with reassurance. “Please... trust me.”

With a deliberate slowness, I opened my eyes, taking in the surroundings, this was my first time seeing without them. Removing them when I was in my previous home was a breeze since it was a family home with no haunting history. Only my parents were tied to the house and at Axiel’s place, I only removed them when I was in the shower or going to bed. Despite this, whenever I didn’t wear them while I was there, I always experienced a comforting sense of ease.

“It’s just you and me here,” he reassured me, “be yourself fully, and let’s make the most of this week.”

Agreeing with a nod, he embraced me, his arms providing a comforting and secure hold. We gazed together as the sun sank below the horizon, leaving behind a canvas of dark blue sky that slowly came alive with the soft glow of the moon.

“Axiel… did you mean it when you called me your girl back at the club?” I questioned

“Of course I did, Vyolette,” he said, immediately, “I mean… if you want to be,”

I smiled and lowered my head shyly, “but, we’re from two different worlds,” I voiced, “in mine, there’s only tragedy, are you sure you want to be a part of that?”

With a swift motion, he turned me around to face him, his eyes fixed on mine, filled with resolute determination. "Believe it or not Vyolette, my world never had meaning until I met you, that first time we met and exchanged pleasantries in the hall, I felt like I had found a part of my soul that was missing," he confessed, his words bringing tears to my eyes, "in my mind—in my heart, you're my reason for existing, and I will never leave your side, I promise you that." Gently, he bent over, causing me to rise on my toes, as our lips met in a passionate, fiery kiss, his lips radiating warmth onto mine.

While I gathered the grocery bags from the trunk, he grabbed our luggage from the back seat and brought them inside. Upon entering the house after him, we were immediately captivated by its tastefully contemporary design. The beauty of the place invoked a strong sense of nostalgia as if it held memories from a past that I couldn't quite recall.

We placed the bags down and took in the spacious layout of the lake house, featuring an open living room, dining room, and kitchen setting, with a cozy lounge area nestled above the kitchen. The house had all the essential amenities—two bathrooms, three bedrooms, and a cozy fireplace in the living room. Additionally, there was a glass room with dirt-ground flooring that provided a stunning view of the lake, complete with a fire pit in the center.

"This place is beautiful Axiel," I said in awe

"I completely agree," he nodded in affirmation. "I was told it runs on solar power, so we don't have to worry about the electricity being cut off or anything, and we get the water from a filtered pump."

I laughed happily, my voice filled with genuine joy, "Honestly, I don't mind moving here after graduation," I expressed, "I feel an indescribable sense of tranquility in this place. Thank you so much for bringing me."

He gave me a shy smile, "You're welcome, Vyolette."

➔NEXT MORNING

For the first time since the accident, I woke up with a sense of peace. While Axiel held me from behind, I planted a soft kiss on his hand, savoring the tenderness of the moment. Looking past the white floral lace curtains beyond the heavy forest-green open curtains on the window, I saw the sun rising above the water, and it was indeed beautiful. The skies and the hills beyond the water were bathed in a vivid orange hue, which mirrored like a radiant star on the water's surface with the bright sun. Despite my efforts to rouse Axiel, he remained in a blissful state of sleep, oblivious to the captivating sight outside our bedroom window.

I quickly slipped into a cozy robe and exited the room, making my way onto the deck to bask in the breathtaking view of the morning sun—a sight that was made even more enchanting than the clear, starry sky from the previous night. However, I couldn't help but appreciate how equally stunning the lake house looked in the daylight.

The water nearby was so transparent that it acted like a mirror, reflecting the home and the tall, imposing pine trees that loomed behind it. The deck, though small, accommodated a roofed-decked speedboat positioned at the edge. I expected Axiel to wake up and come join me, but as the sun climbed higher in the sky, my concern for his prolonged sleep deepened.

I hurried into the room, and as I entered, I saw him lying there motionless, deep in slumber. Worried, I approached and checked for the rise and fall of his chest, only to find it absent. Without hesitation, I climbed into the bed and embraced him tightly, a wave of fear enveloping me. "Axiel, wake up!" I cried, desperately shaking him, feeling his slightly cold skin against my chest. “Oh my God, Axiel, you’re scaring me. Please, please wake up.”

Just as I was about to check his breathing and administer CPR, his eyes suddenly opened, and he gazed up at me with a groggy expression. “Vyolette, what’s the matter?” he asked in a raspy voice.

With tears streaming down my face, I sniffled and wiped them away, finding solace as I tightly embraced him. “You wouldn’t wake up,” I cried, my voice trembling with fear, “I thought something had happened, I thought you were—”

“Hey, hey, I’m here,” he said, his voice filled with concern, his hand gently cupping my face and guiding my gaze to meet his. “I’m sorry I scared you,” he continued, “I guess my body was just making up for the lack of sleep. I haven’t slept since we left the hospital, and it finally caught up with me.”

My sobs echoed through the room as I struggled to put on a smile, but it was no use. “Please,” I pleaded, sniffling, “don’t ever scare me like that again.”

“Hey, I won’t,” he reassured me, his voice filled with warmth as he pulled me into a tight embrace, comforting me. “I... won’t...”

We luxuriated in bed for a few more hours, enjoying the lazy morning before finally deciding to whip up a tasty lunch. In the late afternoon, around 3:30 pm, when the sun's intensity had diminished, we embarked on a hike along a picturesque trail that led us to a breathtaking mountain vista. I was under the impression that we had the woods all to ourselves until I glimpsed a couple of individuals who appeared to be college students making their way down a nearby trail. I suggested we go say hi, but Axiel declined, citing the impending darkness as a reason to head back.

As the night settled in, we huddled around the crackling fire in the area with floor-length glass windows, savoring the taste of melted chocolate and marshmallows, while enthusiastically jotting down a list of activities for our week stay, which I couldn't wait to check off.

CHAPTER ELEVEN

SEE US CONNECT

A WEEK LATER
VYOLETTE

The living room had a cozy ambiance, with dim lighting of the fool moon escaping through the blinds and Axiel and I lounging on a large red faux fur rug. Pillows and cushions surrounded us, and a warm brown blanket kept our feet snug. The crackling fireplace emitted a flickering light, adding to the comforting atmosphere. “The week went by so quickly, didn’t it?” I remarked, mesmerized by the fireplace lighting up the living room, as I sank into Axiel’s lap, feeling his intense gaze on me instead of the cozy view.

“That’s what happens when you’re having fun, and ignoring the outside world in complete isolation,” he chuckled, nodding in agreement. "By the way, have I ever mentioned how mesmerizing your eyes are?"

I felt a rush of warmth in my cheeks as I blushed. "You've mentioned it once or twice," I responded

"Vyolette..." As he called my name, there was a hint of seriousness in his tone, showing that he had something important to say.

My heart pounded in my chest, and a wave of unease washed over me, the cause unknown. "Yes?" I answered, my voice unsure of what he would say next.

"Do you want me to be with you, always?" he asked, his voice filled with uncertainty and vulnerability. "I don't know if you feel the same way that I do, but I can't bear the thought of not being with you. Your presence illuminates my life like nothing else."

"Axiel…" I mumbled

During our first night there, I bravely posed the question to him, and despite him giving me a response, no true confirmation was made. It was clear to me that he desired an official relationship between us, but my hesitation stemmed from the fear of not only putting him in harm's way, but his parents not accepting me since we're not from the same social class.

"However, I feel like I'm being selfish with you," he continued, "I want you to be happy, but I… my mind… my body won't let you go."

"Axiel, I want to be with you, too," I replied, "I—"

"That's not what I mean Vyolette," he interrupted, his voice calm yet worrying.

"Then what is it?" I replied, confused, finally sitting up to face him directly. "Is there something you want to tell me?"

For a moment, his eyes lingered on the fireplace before us, before he briefly glanced back at me. "Nevermind," he said nonchalantly with a defeated sigh, brushing me off in the process, "Not just yet, but if by any chance you're ready for it... I'd love to take you to the prom. If you'd be willing."

I smiled at him, my eyes crinkling with warmth. "Of course I will!"

His intense gaze never wavered as he uttered my name, "Vyolette,"

I've never been to any of the dances at our school before, but this one is special. I'll finally be going, and to make it even better, I'll be going with someone I have strong feelings for. The thought of it makes me genuinely excited. Knowing it was our final night at the lake house and with prom just around the corner, a wave of excitement washed over me as I resolved to make it a night to remember.

"What time are we leaving tomorrow?" I asked, nervously. "I still need to get a dress for the prom."

"Don't worry about that," he said, "I already got something for you."

I admire all he's done and does for me, but sometimes I feel like he's doing too much and I'm afraid to tell him that. "Axiel... I still have money saved up from my previous job," I said, "I could have bought the dress myself."

"Didn't you say that you want to go to college?" he questioned, "You can save your money for then."

"Axiel, we can lease an apartment close to whichever college we choose and live together, and I'll find another job close to it," I responded. "I admire all that you do for me, but sometimes—"

"Vyolette," he cut me off, eyes staring deeply into my soul once again, "as much as I want to—wish to—I'm not always going to be there for you."

"Axiel, where is this coming from? " Confusion filled my voice as I asked.

"I… I'm sorry, I didn't mean it that way," he apologized

I took a moment to ponder his words, letting them sink in. "Axiel, are you sure there's something you're not telling me?" I asked with a concerned tone, full of worry.

His eyes remained downcast as he sighed, creating an uncomfortable silence between us. "My parents will only be gone for a little over a year," he stated, "I just want to make sure that you have everything you need… in case they don't accept you,"

Strangely, I felt like that was not what he intended to say. I tried pressing him on it, but he wouldn't budge. "I have a feeling you're lying to me Axiel," I voiced, "are you?"

I became wary when he didn't respond to my question right away, causing doubt to creep in. "Come," he said, taking my hand and setting me to sit between his legs, his arms wrapped around me, keeping me as warm as the fire. "Vyolette... there's something I need to tell you," he said, his tone heavy with sorrow.

In an instant, a vivid beam of light appeared, and a surge of energy pulsed through my chest, taking me by surprise. An unknown heat came over my body. I felt like the room was engulfed in flames and pulled myself away from Axiel's embrace, he asked me what was wrong but I couldn't respond, my breathing increased and I stood on my feet as I stripped myself of the long-sleeved, button-down boyfriend sleep-shirt nightdress I had on, the only thing remaining being my black lace underwear.

I turned to him, and he stared at me with a puzzled expression. "Vyolette... what are you doing? Is everything alright? Are you feeling okay?" he asked, his voice filled with concern, eyes winding when they met mine. "Your eyes... they're practically glowing white."

"Axiel," I spoke, "I feel… I feel so hot,"

"I'll get you some water," he said, rushing to his feet. With a firm grip, I tackled him to the floor, the force of our collision reverberating with a resounding thud in the space. Sitting up once more, I kept him pinned beneath me, his hands tightly gripping my arms, asking me if I was okay. "You're not burning up or anything," he stated

With each passing moment, his intense gaze into my eyes quickened the pace of my racing heart. Succumbing to the overwhelming feeling, I boldly grabbed his neck, relishing the sensation of his lips against my tongue. "What did you want to say to me?" I asked, my voice carrying a soft and melodic tone.

He remained silent for a moment, and I felt his body quiver under me. "What's going on Vyolette?" he questioned, ignoring my question.

"Axiel…" I called his name sweetly, feeling a sudden drunkenness come over me, a slow, burning sensation above my left breast. "I want you to take me Axiel… my knight…"

"Vyolette I—"

"Do you not want me?" I spoke again, not feeling like the words were my own, "Now is the time to become one with me, my knight… I need my knight… tonight."

AXIEL

The sudden change in Vyolette puzzled me, but only for a moment. I could suddenly sense the strong desire she felt to have me, I could feel it too. It was taking every ounce of willpower I had in me to fight against the powerful urge that was consuming me to have her, the harder I fought against it, the more a sudden pain on the left side of my chest grew. However, given my present state, I was uncertain if I could even meet her expectations, despite what I was feeling.

She leaned down on top of me, her lips leaving a burning sensation on the nape of my neck. I groaned, only feeling a lingering glee in the pain. "Of course I want you, Vyolette," I whispered in her ear, my voice filled with longing.

Contemplating whether to disclose what I've been withholding, I questioned if I should tell her now, or wait until after prom as I had initially planned on doing. As she stared at me, her violet eyes now as white as I had seen them once before, I decided not to. Once again, she cupped my cheeks, her eyes fixated on mine, intensifying the connection between us. Succumbing to the overwhelming urge, I gently brushed my lips against hers and then kissed her passionately. The more our passion intensified, the more I felt an agonizing sensation as if my arm were being scraped with a heated needle, but my desire for Vyolette's touch overwhelmed any pain.

She desperately removes my shirt, her movements against my lips rough and dominating. "Have me, my knight," she said, as I held her waist.

...⦸...

The moment her words reached my ears, a wave of disorientation washed over me as though my body was being taken over by some external force. "Okay... I'll try," I replied. With a slow and deliberate motion, I guided Vyolette down onto the soft rug, positioning myself between her legs. My eyes locked onto her, as she stared at me with a hunger that words couldn't express.

I sat up, removed my T-shirt, and effortlessly tossed it to the side before leaning my bare body down on top of her. I showered her neck, chest, and body with gentle, peppery kisses, causing her to arch in anticipation as I moved my lips toward the edge of her underwear before helping her out of them. Lying on the rug before me, completely naked, her long black hair flowed beneath her like a veil. My senses were overwhelmed by the allure of her perfect figure, leaving me yearning to become one with her. But why?

Moving back up her body, I can sense the warmth of her hand tracing my bare chest, her nails grazing my skin as they roamed lower, playfully pulling on the band of my boxers. When her hand slipped inside, a sharp gasp eluded her lips.

"Your appearance makes no justice for your size," she commented, a smile spreading across her lips.

She grabbed onto it and squeezed it once, and it immediately stiffened. At that moment, my willpower disintegrated, and I lost control of my body once more and forcefully shoved my tongue down her throat—she accepted me instantly. I grazed my hand down the shape of her waist, my fingers lingering against her wetness for a moment as she moved her waist in a circular motion against my hand. As she lets out a soft moan, I increase the speed of my fingers, sending waves of pleasure coursing through her.

She beckoned me to take her, and I stopped what I was doing, positioning my body on top of her, my member at her pulsing entrance. Slowly, I slid inside her, and she let out a sharp gasp, biting her lip and moaning, her fingers digging into my forearm as I began thrusting slowly.

"Axiel," she moaned, the passion between us intensifying as we became one.

With her nails digging into my back and grazing my sides, I pushed myself to go harder, relishing the sensation of her legs wrapped tightly around my waist. Our moans of ecstasy reverberated through the house, intensifying the passion and the connection between us. I buried my face in her neck, wanting to bite her, but not pushing my luck in doing so.

Her cries of pleasure grew louder and louder and continued to echo through the thick walls of the house until I pressed my lips against hers, engulfing her in another passionate kiss. Moving my waist with a rhythm as I looked down at her, the white glow in her eyes slowly faded and they regained their violet hue.

"I love you, Vyolette White," I muttered

She smiled back at me, her words coming out in a monotone whisper. "I love you too, my knight… Axiel Knightly,"

CHAPTER TWELVE

SEE US DANCE

VYOLETTE

My mind was elsewhere as I drove back home with Axiel, the sights and sounds of the road fading into the background. My memory of last night was hazy at best, but I recalled having an out-of-body experience and the throbbing ache in my muscles below left no doubt about what had transpired. Upon awakening this morning, I found myself disrobed, nestled in Axiel's embrace, cocooned beneath a large quilt on top of the faux fur rug, while the fireplace sat extinguished in front of us. I remained unfazed until I heard the unnaturally slow beating of his heart.

Just before we left, I contemplated asking him about it, but my ambivalence towards knowing the answer made me hesitate. Axiel called my name, bringing me out of my trail of thought, but said nothing when I responded.

With a slight adjustment of my glasses, I pondered the idea of deviating from our route and making a stop at the hospital so he could receive a thorough check-up. My worry for him only grew when I saw him slowly drifting, as though he was going to pass out.

"Axiel, are you okay?" I asked

"Yeah, I'm fine," he replied, "nothing a little rest can't fix,"

"Are you sure?" I pressed.

He reassured me he was fine, but I couldn't shake off my unease. Another half hour later, I parked the car in his garage and we entered his home, each carrying our bags. In complete silence, he made a beeline for his bedroom and closed the door behind him, leaving me with a mix of concern and curiosity. Although I wanted to go and see how he was doing, his previous response made me give him the space in which he needed time to rest.

Upon entering my room, I nonchalantly dropped my bag near the door. However, when I looked up, I was taken aback by the sight of a breathtaking, beautiful prom dress, delicately encased in a clear gown bag and hanging on my closet door. *'Was this the dress Axiel said he'd gotten for me?* I questioned, running my fingers along the intricate stitching over the gown bag.

The dress was absolutely stunning and sophisticated, and to make it even better, it was my favorite color. The dress was a vintage lavender tulle lilac applique beaded with lace ruffles, a silk trim, and a thigh-high split. The sight of the dress and the matching two-inch strapped heels he had gotten me brought a smile to my face, but my worries quickly dampened my mood. Reflecting on it, Axiel had been behaving oddly ever since the accident, and I couldn't help but wonder if it had taken a greater toll on him than I initially thought.

With the dress safely back where it belonged, I settled onto my bed, propping a pillow between my legs as I mulled over what to do next. The notion crossed my mind that Axiel had passed away in the accident, and I was now sharing my existence with his ghost, but I promptly rejected the idea. For six years, I coexisted with the ethereal presence of my parents, and to make physical contact with them, it took intense concentration. Their embraces were cold to the touch, but they brought a sense of warmth and comfort to my heart. They found themselves completely devoid of lifting anything, no matter how much effort they exerted, nor could they consume food, and I could not see them when I had my glasses on. And what I believed happened last night definitely wouldn't have happened. Axiel ticked all the boxes of not being a wandering spirit.

Regardless of the circumstances, something was definitely wrong. "He promised he would never leave me, but was that because he knew I could see him after he's gone?" I questioned myself, tears flowing down my face as I cried myself to sleep.

'Vyolette… Vyolette…'

Startled by the sudden knock on my door, I heard someone calling out, "Vyolette…? Are you ready yet?"

"No, not yet," I responded, groggy and rubbing the sleep from my eyes. "I'll be down in a few minutes,"

Jumping out of bed, I raced to the bathroom, where I quickly turned the cold shower on and diligently lathered my body, feeling the refreshing water awaken my senses. Getting myself ready, I slipped into the dress which fit me perfectly—it puzzled me that Axiel not only got a dress in my favorite color but my size as well. As I ran my hands down the fabric, I could feel its softness against my skin.

Ready to leave, I made my way downstairs, the rhythmic clicking of my heels echoing on the wooden tiles with each step. As I glanced down the stairs, I spotted Axiel leaning against the beam, his relaxed posture giving away his confidence. When he heard me coming, he turned around, his eyes widening in astonishment as he saw me, his face flushing red.

"You look amazing, Vyolette," he stated, "The color truly suits you."

'So that's why he got it,' I thought to myself.

After reaching the bottom of the stairs, I couldn't take my eyes off him. His black suit was a perfect complement to my dress, with the matching undershirt and tie tying our outfits together. He excused himself for a minute and brought back a small glass box with a matching lavender wrist corsage set made of lavender daisies and white roses.

Once he secured the wrist corsage on my wrist, I carefully attached his corsage to the lapel of his tuxedo jacket, savoring the tender kiss he planted on my cheek before holding my hand. "Shall we go?" he spoke

My face lit up with a smile as I gazed up at him. "Yeah…"

ଔ…

Upon arriving at the prom, which was being held at the Phoenix banquet hall, Axiel wasted no time in suggesting we take a seat at a secluded table in the back since I hadn't been here before and didn't want to be noticed by the other students, I agreed. Besides, I had a feeling Rejanae and her clique would harass us if they saw us, and I had no desire to engage with her and let them spoil our evening.

The color theme of purple, pink, and gold created a visually stunning atmosphere in the hall. Welcoming the students was a photo area that exuded charm, boasting an enchanting balloon-floral-vine arch in shades of gold, purple, and pink. Adjacent to it across the hall, a lavish buffet table beckoned with an array of mouthwatering finger foods and an assortment of drinks stacked high and ready to be enjoyed. The dance floor was surrounded by tables in every corner, providing a narrow walkway for students and chaperones. The hall was bathed in a magical glow, courtesy of the starry disco balls and white Christmas lights adorning the ceiling, a live band singing and entertaining the students.

I got us each a glass of fruit punch and brought it back to our tables, this was the only thing I intended to consume here since I don't eat food I don't cook myself—a rule my parents had always insisted I follow. When I got back to our table, I placed his drink in front of him and sat down beside him, however, he only stared at his glass looking dejected.

"Axiel, is everything okay?" I asked

"Ah, yeah," he replied, his gaze shifting from his glass before fixing on the couples moving in perfect harmony on the dance floor to the slow, romantic music being played.

"Axiel, would you like to dance?" I asked

"Uh... maybe that's not a good idea," he replied, his voice filled with hesitation, "We should wait till a lively, upbeat song comes on."

"Come on Axiel!" I insisted, hoping that my persistence would break through his funk and bring him back to his usual self. "It's our last day of school before graduation, we should enjoy ourselves."

Noticing his unease, I decided to stop pushing and give him some space and shifted my attention to the couples gracefully moving on the dance floor, taking a sip of my drink.

The unmistakable sound of his cloth-covered chair scraping against the wooden tile caught my attention, and when I looked, I saw him standing tall, his right hand waiting for me to take it.

I looked up at him, confused. "I thought you said—"

Cutting my words short, he confidently declared, "One dance wouldn't hurt."

As I tentatively held his hand, I couldn't help but notice the coolness of his touch. With a firm grip on my waist, he confidently escorted me to the dance floor. I turned to meet his eyes, intertwining my fingers with his and settling my other hand comfortably on his shoulder. With his hand firmly on my waist, he pulled me closer, our foreheads meeting as we swayed to the rhythm of 'Dancing on my own', the male singer singing it with such soul and emotion that I felt it within me.

Ignoring everything and everyone around us, only letting the music guide our bodies, Axiel held me by the tip of my fingers, and with a swift spin, he released me briefly before pulling me back into his arms, this time holding me even closer than before, my back against his chest.

With a beaming smile, I gaze up at him, and we become lost in each other's eyes as we move harmoniously across the dance floor. The room faded away, and all that remained was the synchronized rhythm of our bodies, lost in the spellbinding allure of the music.

"I had no idea you were such a talented dancer," I giggled, feeling the sudden warmth of his embrace as he pulled me closer.

"I've had enough practice growing up thanks to my parents forcing me to balls and banquets," he replied with a soft smile.

With each step we took, it felt as if the room became empty, leaving only the two of us to dance, enwrapped in the music. For a brief moment, I slipped into reality and saw that the other students had retreated to the periphery of the dancefloor, leaving only him and me in the center, dancing away. Their gasps, pointing gestures, and murmurs filled the air, yet my focus remained solely on the euphoria of being wrapped in Axiel's arms, it felt like our feet weren't even touching the ground. The rhythm was so captivating that it made us feel like we could dance the night away.

With a final spin, he drew me towards him, and as our lips connected, a collective gasp filled the room, the lights abruptly flickered on fully lighting up the hall, and the music abruptly stopped, bringing it into immediate silence.

The silence stretched on for a few seconds before someone mustered the courage to speak up, shattering the eerie atmosphere. "What is she doing?"

"She's dancing on her own!" someone answered, clearly shocked.

Breaking apart, I noticed the hall had fallen into complete silence, resembling the stillness of an empty room. Looking up at Axiel, he looked around, fear consuming his expression. "I knew this was a bad idea," he muttered, his voice filled with regret. "I'm sorry I let myself get carried away."

"It's fine, Axiel," I reassured, intertwining my fingers with his and offering a warm smile. "Let's go grab another drink and go back to our seats."

Heading toward the buffet table with Axiel following close behind me, the gazes of the other students and teacher were fixed upon us, their jaws still dropped in astonishment, unable to hide their surprise. '*Why are they acting so shocked?'* I questioned in thought, *'Did Axiel and I overdo it with our dancing?'*

Before we could even reach the punch bowl, Rejanae intercepted us, forcefully pushing me aside with a jolt. "You just had to ruin prom for everyone, didn't you?" she exclaimed, her words laced with a mixture of anger and bitterness. "You and your freaky ghost shit!"

Adjusting my glasses, I couldn't help but feel a sense of confusion as I tried to understand what she was referring to. Yes, I know the school had a few wandering souls, but I've had my glasses on all night and haven't seen any sign of them.

Ignoring her, I walked past, but she wasn't about to let me go that easily. She grabbed my shoulders, her touch firm, and turned me to face her, where she immediately began insulting me. My heart raced and burned, and I felt Axiel's hand close around mine, his firm grip guiding me away from the commotion. Suddenly, Rejanae snatched my glasses from my face, effortlessly broke them, and flung them over my head.

I could feel the anger coursing through my veins, heating my entire body. "What the hell is your problem?" I snapped, delivering a powerful punch that sent her reeling back, colliding with a group of startled students.

"You are!" she snarled, as her friends helped her to her feet. "WAIT! Weren't your eyes gray a second ago?" she questioned, "Why are they white?" she hid her sudden fear behind her unexplained anger, "YOU'RE SUCH A DAMN FREAK!"

Without my glasses, my eyes were violet, not white. Losing my glasses, a cherished item that my grandmother had given me before she passed away, meant that I could no longer perceive the world with the same clarity. I was clueless about where she managed to attain those glasses, and I couldn't find a way to obtain a duplicate pair. Without them, I could never show my face anywhere again, and could only pray that getting back home would be safe sailing.

In my fear-induced haze, I completely missed the fact that the school's wandering souls were mysteriously absent. "Axiel, let's go home," I pleaded, my voice filled with desperation, "I don't want to be here anymore."

"Axiel?" Rejanae said, her voice filled with confusion, as she absentmindedly massaged her jaw and let out a disdainful snort, before crossing her arms. "What, is he here or something? I thought he was in a coma, not dead," she laughed, "cute, you're so desperate—"

"Are you blind!" I cried, my tears mixing with the lingering anger inside me. "Or are you trying to be more of a bitch more than you already are?"

Just as her hand was about to make contact with my face, Axiel yanked me out of harm's way. It was then that I realized her hand passed through him as if he were made of mist. "W-what the hell was that!" she shouted, holding her hand. "W-what was that chill I just felt?"

"That... that can't be," I said, my voice trembling, as I cautiously took a step back. "Axiel... you're… we had… no…"

With a slow, deliberate movement, he turned around and his gaze met mine, causing me to instinctively retreat another step. Confusion and disbelief flooded my mind. We just danced for a long time, was I just dancing on my own the entire time?

"Vyolette," he took a step forward, prompting me to take another step back.

"Wait, you mean you're... you're not actually here?" Stuttering, I hesitantly reached out my hand, almost brushing against his face, but then abruptly pulled back. "You're—you're dead?" I asked in a shaky voice as my eyes welled up.

There was absolutely no way that was possible, was the last two weeks a lie? How long has he been gone? Was it since the accident? How did we become intimate if he was gone? This can't be real, for the past few weeks since the accident, Axiel has done nothing that says he was a ghost, so why couldn't anyone else see him?

"She needs to go to a mental hospital!" Rejanae barked, her words slicing through the air. "Get her!"

Overwhelmed by the sudden realization, my legs gave way, and I crumpled to the floor, immobile. Amidst the crowd, Axiel took a stand in front of me, attempting to halt their progress. Yet, I couldn't comprehend his intentions—how could he affect them if I was the sole witness to his presence? In what way could he intervene and put an end to their intended actions?

"STAY AWAY FROM HER!" he bellowed, his powerful voice resonating through the air, sending everyone and everything around me recoiling from a gust of wind. With an almost inhuman speed, he grabbed my hands and whisked me away towards the exit, my feet not touching the ground.

Inside the car, I refused to acknowledge what was unfolding, tears streaming down my face and causing my vision to become hazy. I pressed a button and the vehicle sprang to life, its engine growling with energy. As he directed me to drive, I swiftly shifted the car into reverse, hurriedly maneuvering out of the parking spot. Without bothering to buckle up, I switched to drive and sped out of the parking lot. I just wanted to be out of there.

The drive back was so quick that it seemed like we were magically transported to the house. Without bothering to turn off the car, I hurried to my room, stumbling over my long dress as I climbed the stairs. Ignoring Axiel's pleas for me to stop and hear him out, I slammed the door shut behind me, the sound of the lock clicking into place sealing me off from his presence.

While turning around to seek solace on my bed and release my emotions through tears, he unexpectedly appeared in front of me. "Vyolette, please," he begged, "let me explain,"

"Explain what?" I retaliated angrily, my voice filled with both confusion and frustration, "That you've been lying to me? That you humiliated me in front of the entire school?"

"I didn't mean to Vyolette," he responded, "I swear, I was going to tell you tonight, I just wanted—"

"You wanted me to look like a fool!" I snapped back, cutting through his words. "How can I touch you, how can I feel you as if you're alive and breathing when you're really dead?"

"Did you attend my funeral?" his question hung in the air, delivered with a surprising blend of anger and composure.

I realized the futility of my ranting and ceased. He's right, I never went to his funeral, and though he couldn't be seen by others, he had a heartbeat—as slow as it was. With my parents, I couldn't hear even a faint beat of their hearts when they held me close, nor did they have the warmth he sometimes radiated. Did that mean he was somewhat alive despite being somewhat dead?

With a sigh, he spoke calmly and reassuringly, "I'm not dead Vyolette, I don't know how you could feel my presence like this, but please, have a seat and let me explain."

With a gentle pat on the bed, he motioned for me to join him. At first, I hesitated, but my curiosity compelled me to sit down and listen to what he had to say, even as I wiped away my tears.

CHAPTER THIRTEEN

SEE WHAT HAPPENED

LATER AFTER THE ACCIDENT

AXIEL

I called for Vyolette, but I couldn't hear her, I couldn't see her, and since the first day I met her, I couldn't sense her. Stretching out before me was a dark road, twisting and turning like a ribbon of asphalt vanishing into the distance toward a bright white orb. My body was hit by an electric surge, and my eyes flickered open for just an instant. The darkness held me captive for a moment, but a faint glimmer of awareness fought to break through, like a dying flame refusing to be extinguished.

"He's back!" someone shouted

When I opened my eyes again, the rhythmic beeping of monitors filled the room, while doctors and nurses hurriedly attended to a motionless patient on a gurney. The doctors and nurses spoke hastily, their instructions and commands overlapping in a cacophony of uncertainty. I then saw a doctor lean over to a nurse and whisper, "Make sure they understand the severity of his internal injuries and the slim chances of recovery."

Wandering why I was in the hospital room of a stranger, I cautiously took a step closer and was shocked to see that I was the one lying on the bed. My face was bloodied, but as it was wiped off by a nurse, no cuts or wounds were seen, "Oh no, is that Vyolette's blood?" I gasped.

"No, it's your blood," a woman with a soft voice answered, her words laced with desperation. "You're dying... but we can't let that happen."

As I turned around, my eyes landed on a pair of figures I recognized instantly. There stood a young woman, appearing to be in her mid-twenties, her long jet-black hair flowing down her shoulders. She was elegantly dressed in a white lace midi dress. Beside her stood a guy of the same age, his hair short, but just as black, wearing a white long-sleeved loungewear.

"You're Vyolette's parents… I saw you the night I first dropped her off," I said, taking note that they were not in the same attire they had the first night I saw them. "Am I dead?"

"No..." answered Vyolette's father, "for now, you're just ...sleeping."

"You took a lot of damage protecting Vyolette," her mother added, "thank you,"

"Wait, did you just say you saw us?" her father questioned, "when we lived with her?"

"Yeah," I replied, "you two were on the front porch waiting on her,"

They locked eyes with each other before turning their gaze back to me, curiosity evident in their expressions. They asked if I possessed the same ability as Vyolette to see the departed, to which I replied in the negative. I believed it was a one-time thing because I never encountered them again after that—until now.

I turned back to my motionless body, which they had now transferred to a hospital bed. "But my body looks fine," I voiced, "where did all that blood come from?"

"On the outside, your wounds have all healed," her father stated, "but on the inside, since they separated you from Vyolette, it will take a while longer,"

"Why am I here then," I questioned, "Why are you here? And if you've always been here, why can't Vyolette see you?"

"Vyolette finally let us go, she doesn't need us anymore," her mother stated, "but we came back because it's her eighteenth birthday, and we couldn't protect her,"

"I don't understand," I said, confused.

"There's something you need to know about Vyolette," her mother said as she walked closer to me, her hands clasped in front of her.

"If it's about her seeing ghosts, then I already know about it," I voiced, and I don't care, "I love her nonetheless and want to be with her."

Her mother shook her head and approached me, "it's not that," she claimed before she started explaining, "Vyolette was told by her assigned psychologist that the accident caused her to see the dead, but that's not entirely true."

"What do you mean?" I queried.

"Seeing the dead is in her blood, and it goes beyond just that—far beyond than you could comprehend," her father spoke, "It's been in my family's generation for centuries, but it skipped me and my mother. The accident only caused her powers to awaken early though not fully, but the necromancy eyes did, the shock and trauma of the accident activated it before my mother could tell her about it, and could help her control it." she continued, "If she didn't go through another trauma before she turned eighteen, it would have gone dormant again, but it's too late now, it's already awakened and the connection I believe you two share, have made it impossible to get rid of."

"I… I don't understand," I said, confused. "What are you guys talking about?"

It's true, I felt an inexplicable pull towards Vyolette from the moment we crossed paths, one that I struggled to put into words. However, it seemed like her parents understood this connection on a much deeper level, something I couldn't fully comprehend. I asked for proper clarity and they did so willingly, as the doctors and nurses tended to my physical body.

Vyolette's parents divulged to me that their family possessed an extraordinary gift, which her father reluctantly labeled as a curse after the tragedy that befell his older sister when she turned eighteen. Consequently, when they found out Vyolette carried it, they made it their mission to safeguard her from encountering a similar fate by keeping her sheltered—her grandmother was against it, but understood since she had lost her only daughter.

On the night of the accident, they received a chilling warning that they were being followed, intensifying their urgency to get Vyolette to the lake house for safety. However, their plans were abruptly disrupted by the unexpected occurrence of the accident, leaving them with the grim realization that they were specifically targeted.

"Axiel, you should know that Vyolette is more connected to the supernatural world than this one," her father stated, "due to the accidents and the trauma that followed, her powers will only grow uncontrolled, so we need you to take her to a certain place, a secluded area where you can teach her how to control them before its too late."

I forced a laugh, there was no way they could be serious. "You want me to do what?"

"We have a lake house in a secluded area in the woods, it's specially guarded, so humans can't get through the entrance nor any of the barriers and there is a safety mechanism that will keep a certain type of people out unless welcomed," her mother said, "Take her there and teach her to control her powers, or at least for a week so they can go back dormant until your physical body is fully healed,"

"How do you expect me to get through if you just said humans can't?" I questioned, "Is it because of our connection?"

"Yes," he answered, "we don't know why ourselves, but you two share something that we ourselves can't understand,"

"When we saw you two in the accident, something happened Axiel," her mother explained, her voice tinged with anxiety. "Since our house was destroyed by that fire set by those high schoolers, we've been keeping a close eye on Vyolette, especially tonight. When we saw them ram you off the road, we were eager to help, but something happened—Vyolette caused something to happen." She looked in the direction of my physical body, "that's why your wounds have all healed, and your internal wounds are slowly healing,"

Suddenly, a nurse walked in with some documents on a clipboard, "Doctor Ballen, Mr. and Mrs. Knightly want him moved to the private section and request to have an NDA signed by everyone who tended to him," she stated, "There's something else…"

"They're my parents go again," I said to myself

"Wait, your last name is knightly?" said her father

"Yeah… why?" I responded.

Her father laughed, "We tried so hard to keep our families apart, but in the end, our kids still crossed paths,"

"What…?"

"Maybe it was fate," her mother said, her voice calm and welcoming. "Sometimes, no matter how hard we try, we can't escape the path set out for us."

"With them being your parents, you should have no issue getting through the barrier," her father stated

Despite my inquiry about how they knew my parents, they paid no attention to me and swiftly steered the conversation towards Vyolette's predicament, stressing the heightened threat she now faced. Against my better judgment, I agreed to do as they said, considering Vyolette had already allowed them to stay beyond their welcome and understanding that the end result wouldn't be favorable, as they had informed me.

"How long am I gonna be out for?" I questioned

"We don't know," her mother answered, "could be a few days or even a month."

"Or with you being so far away from Vyolette, there's a slim possibility you won't," her father added

Vyolette's parents gave me a lot to think about. I took a bated breath, the thought of not making it through broke me. From the accident her parents described and how they said my car looked at the bottom of the hill, I should have been dead. '*What exactly did Vyolette do to cause all my wounds to heal so quickly?*' Vyolette's parents left and I followed the nurses as they brought my body up to the private section of the hospital. Each passing day, I continued to be immobile by my bedside, relentlessly exploring every idea that came to mind in my quest to reenter my physical self. With each passing day, I held onto the hope that my parents would show up and check on me, but as a week went by, my optimism began to wane. The nurse my parents had assigned by the hospital to care for me was the only person who entered and exited my room.

Looking at my body, I brushed a lock of hair away from my face. Surprised I was able to do so, I looked at my hand when her parents appeared in front of me. "Axiel, Vyolette is being discharged," her mother said.

"What?" I cried, "I haven't woken up yet,"

I wanted to see her before she left, I didn't know how long it would be again until my body fully healed and I was pulled back into it, and I didn't want to roam too far from my physical body. When I reached her room, I stood outside, watching her carefully place her glasses on before I entered—I didn't want her to see me, not in this state, I only wanted to be near her for a moment before she left. As I phased through the door, Vyolette turned to face it and her eyes grew wide in disbelief.

"Axiel, you're ok!" she cried

With a burst of energy, she dashed towards me, and I held her tightly in a warm hug, gently kissing her neck, inhaling deeply to relish her long-missed fragrance. "*I thought I'd lost you*!" We say in sync.

Our brief laughter filled the space between us, and as I leaned in, our lips met in a tender kiss. I then rested my head against hers, feeling a sense of contentment, and couldn't help but smile. The sound of her father clearing his throat snapped me back to reality, reminding me of the predicament I was in. She then excused herself for a moment and closed the blinds of the room, giving us much-needed privacy.

"The doctor said you were in a coma," she cried, "I was about to come see you,"

"I'm here now," I replied confidently, my words echoing with a sense of permanence.

Her eyes were filled with tears, sparkling as they escaped and ran down her cheeks. I watched as she lifted her glasses to wipe them away, and in that moment, I saw a hint of fear flicker across her face. At first, I thought she had seen her parents, but that wasn't the case—we were at a hospital after all, and I recalled her telling me what happened the last time she was there.

"Let's go home," I said, wrapping my arms around her.

"Please let's..." she agreed

Exiting the hospital, we were met with lingering gazes from the staff. As I pulled her closer, I couldn't help but notice the forced smile on her face, a poignant reminder of my desire to never leave her side. "Don't pay attention to them," I whispered, walking with her down the hall and toward the exit.

"Is it okay to let her leave?" A nurse softly whispered as we walked past them.

Vyolette's ability to perceive me, embrace me, and kiss me left me conflicted. Knowing she wouldn't be able to see me without her glasses, I bided my time before entering. But now that she sees me despite having them on, I found myself unable to leave her side.

⇢⇢⇢BACK TO THE PRESENT

Since the last night at the lake house, I've been feeling incredibly fatigued, as if my energy is slowly seeping away from me. I thought I could make it through prom without revealing the truth—and since Vyolette and I were always the unseen ones of the school, I thought we would go unnoticed, but my plan completely backfired, leaving me in a mess. In the end, I ended up unwillingly doing to Vyolette the thing she dreaded most.

"You knew you weren't physically there with me, and you never told me!" Vyolette's voice was filled with anger as she sobbed. "How could you do that to me, Axiel?"

I tried to hold her, but she pushed me away, "You saw my parents after the fire and said nothing—you knew how much I've missed them. How could you!?"

"I made a mistake, Vyolette!" I responded, "They told me not to! I thought I was protecting you by not saying anything."

Her words rumbled through the air, filled with confusion and disbelief. It was all a jumble of confusion to her—nothing seemed to make any sense. Finally, allowing me to hold her, I embraced her as she sobbed uncontrollably in my arms, wiping the tears from her glimmering eyes that were now colored pearl, I apologized profusely.

"You can't be gone Axiel," she cried, punching my chest, "I need you with me,"

"And I will be Vyolette," I responded

"Not like this," she shook her head, bawling her eyes out. "Please not like this, I can't go through this again."

Suddenly, her parents appeared in the room, "Axiel, something's wrong," her father said, "an unauthorized person entered your room and now you're flatlining."

They were right, as I could feel the shockwave I felt the night I arrived at the hospital. "I don't have much time Vyolette," I stated

"W—what do you mean?" She asked

Losing my balance, I fell backward, and she quickly grabbed hold of me to prevent me from falling. As I raised my hands to my face, I noticed it fading in and out of my vision, leaving me disoriented. Vyolette's concerned voice asked me what was happening, but I remained silent, unable to provide an answer. Was this always supposed to happen? Was this the reason I've been feeling drained? Was this the moment where I was facing the reality of my impending demise? I wanted to keep my promise, I wanted to stay at her side always, but not like this.

"Don't leave me Axiel!" she cried, wrapping her hands tightly around me, forcing me out of my trail of thought.

I pulled her closer into a comforting embrace as I ran my hands through her hair, kissing her lightly, "No matter what Vyolette… know that I love you, and I'll always be by your side," I confessed

Her tears left her eyes like a never-ending river. "Please don't leave me Axiel, please!" she begged, "You're all I have, please don't go!"

I didn't want to leave her, but what choice did I have? I could sense my body slipping away, the constant flatline of the monitor echoing in my ears, while the doctors desperately tried to revive me, their efforts proving futile. It became evident that the internal injuries were more serious than I initially thought and whoever entered my room only sped up the process of my death.

"Vyolette," I forced to speak, holding her face with one hand as she cradled me in her arms, "you have the most beautiful pearl eyes I've ever seen…"

"NO, NO, NO!" she cried, her eyes glowing as she embraced me tighter, "Axiel, I'm begging you, please don't abandon me. I'm pleading with you, please stay. YOU PROMISED! PLEASE YOU PROMISED YOU'D NEVER LEAVE ME!"

"I'm sorry… Vyolette," I forced my words, "promise me, you'll live on, promise me,"

She shook her head, still sobbing out of control. "I don't want to, not without you, please."

"I'm sorry, Vyolette…"

In an instant, a powerful force tugged at me, and a brilliant light engulfed my senses. As I scoped my surroundings, I saw

I was now back in my hospital room. The doctor and two nurses stood by my side, their disappointed faces suggesting that their efforts to resuscitate me had not been fruitful.

The doctor looked at his watch and sighed. *'Time of death, 11:59 pm,'*

'Axiel… Axiel…' Vyolette's voice echoed through the room of my mind, 'you can't go Axiel… AXIELLLL!'

A bright light suddenly engulfed the room.

CHAPTER FOURTEEN

DON'T LEAVE ME

VYOLETTE

The moment Axiel disappeared in my arms, I felt a triggering, broken sensation shoot through my entire body. His departure shattered the trust I had built in him, leaving me to wonder why he deceived me after assuring me he would always be by my side. I tried to reassure myself that maybe I was dreaming, maybe this was all a nightmare, but as the icy wind howled through the bedroom window, sending a chill through my body, doubt crept in.

"No, no, no," I repeated, my heart sinking. "He wouldn't break his promise, would he?" The wind howled around me, its intensity increasing by the second, causing my thoughts to swirl uncontrollably. Suddenly, a sharp pain shot through my neck, plunging me into darkness.

"Axiel…"

Slowly, my consciousness returned to me and I found myself in my room—the guestroom at Axiel's place. Opening my eyes, I took in my surroundings and spotted a young woman sitting on a chair next to my bed, completely absorbed in scrolling through her phone.

"You're awake," she said, "normally, I would ask what you're doing here, but from the way you kept calling for my son while you were seemly unconscious, I could come up with a proper theory,"

"Axiel, where is he?" I questioned, looking around frantically.

As she rested her hand on my shoulder, I felt the gentle pressure urging me to recline. "He's in the hospital," she replied, "but—"

"No, he was here," I cried, "I was—he was here, I was just holding him,"

"No," she said sternly, "he's in the hospital right now and has been there for two weeks, why would you think he was here?"

A sudden pulse coursed through my body, and I grabbed hold of my chest as the voice of Axiel calling my name echoed in my mind. At that moment, I accepted reality, Axiel wasn't with me that day I left the hospital—if that was the case, why could I see him when I was certain I was wearing my glasses? I touched my face and recalled Rejanae breaking my glasses, but I remembered wearing them the day I left the hospital. Were the doctors telling the truth when they said he was in a coma, was that why I could see him despite wearing my glasses?

"Hey, did you hear what I said?" she gave me a slight shake to get my attention.

"I… I need to go see him," I ignored her, climbing out of bed and stumbling over the skirt of the dress. "I want to go see Axiel, I need to go see him,"

"First, you need to calm down," said the woman, "I don't need my home being blown to smithereens."

I stared at her, extremely confused, "…what?"

Feeling a sense of confusion, I promptly apologized. After helping me to my feet, she kindly asked if I wanted to change clothes, but I declined, my sole focus being on seeing Axiel. At first, I wondered who the woman was, but when I took a good look at her, I realized she was Axiel's mother and the man shouting her name, 'Jade' from downstairs, was his father.

Racing upstairs, the man burst into the room, his voice trembling, to share the devastating update—the doctors had called, stating that Axiel had passed, and they had to go retrieve his body. The realization of Axiel's predicament left me paralyzed, and I found myself being carried to the car by his father, his mother trailing behind with a worried expression. The passing streetlights and the constant stream of vehicles during our drive to the hospital gave me an eerie feeling, as if I was experiencing an out-of-body phenomenon.

'*Axiel, you can't be gone*,' I kept muttering to myself.

Glancing into the rearview mirror, I caught his father stealing a quick, curious look at me while skillfully navigating through the busy road, surpassing the speed limit. His mother was engrossed in her phone, her fingers dancing across the screen as if typing an urgent message. I found it puzzling that they didn't ask any questions. Additionally, I wondered if they knew I was at their house since they knew Axiel's whereabouts, but still went home. And what did they do to me?

"Young lady, what is your name?" his father finally asked, peering at me through the rearview mirror.

"Vyolette," I answered, fidgeting with the broken nail on my thumb, "Vyolette White,"

"What?" his mother gasped, "as in the daughter of Viola and Hamlet?"

"You know my parents?" I questioned

She snorted a short laugh, responding yet still ignoring my question. "Wow,"

In a rush, he drove into the hospital parking lot, and without waiting for the car to come to a complete stop, I leaped out, tugged up my dress, and sprinted into the hospital. Despite the doctors and nurses urgently screaming for me to stop and requesting security, I continued and entered the staircase, determined to reach Axiel. With each step towards the top floor, my heart raced in my chest, the pulsations resembling a radar signal, guiding me towards Axiel.

Upon arriving at the floor where Axiel's room was, I was confronted by two towering, muscular men dressed in black, their shades so dark I could see my reflection in them. "Sorry miss, no one is allowed in except for Mr. and Mrs. Knightly," one of them said, resting his hand on my chest.

My eyes locked onto his hand, filled with anger, as I swiftly grabbed hold of it and twisted it in a painful backward motion. "Get out of my way!" I growled

With a firm grip on my arm, the other guy's voice carried a menacing undertone, "Young lady, you do not want us to hurt—"

I glared at him, my anger boiling over as I couldn't bear being kept away from Axiel any longer. "Get away! Get away! GET AWAY!" I exploded.

"*I want you to believe in yourself, Vyolette...*" his words resonated in my mind, "*You're stronger than you think.*"

Without warning, an invisible force yanked the men away from me, leaving me with an opportunity to enter the room. I stopped running and my heart dropped as I gazed upon the motionless figure of Axiel, lying on the hospital bed, disconnected from any life-sustaining machines.

"No, Axiel... you can't be dead," I cried, my voice trembling, as I rushed to his side. I dropped myself onto his lifeless body, feeling the coldness seep into my touch. Tears streamed down my face, overwhelmed by the bitter reality I couldn't grasp. I couldn't understand why he was taken away from me—it just didn't seem fair. "You promised…"

"My knight," I said, rising to my feet, as a strange sensation washed over me, making me feel detached from my own body. It felt surreal as if I was floating outside my own body. Just like the last night at the lake house, I observed my hand leaning over Axiel's lifeless form, gently parting his lips with my index finger and placing a hand on his still chest, directly over his heart. Leaning in, our lips connected, and I witnessed a luminous white orb traverse from my heart, up my throat, and into his mouth, casting a brilliant glow upon reaching his heart. "We are now fully connected as one, my knight," my voice said in a soft, monotonous tone.

I was abruptly snapped back into my body, and a whirlwind of dizziness engulfed me. When I saw Axiel's lifeless body on the bed, the room filled with the sound of my desperate sobs. I clung to him, pleading for him to come back to me, not wanting to accept that he was gone. "Axiel, please," I cried, "don't leave me. I can't bear to say goodbye."

"He's gone, Vyolette," said Jade, her voice filled with sorrow. I looked back and saw her standing at the door, her husband's comforting hand on her shoulder. "Say your goodbyes to him so we can have his body moved," she said sternly.

"NO!" I cried, "Axiel is not gone, he's… he's sleeping, he's just sleeping."

Her approach was quiet, and I felt the warmth of her hand as it settled gently on my shoulder. "Vyolette—"

"I said he's not dead!" I shouted, and the force of my voice caused her to instinctively retreat a few steps. While she may be his mom, the pain I'm feeling surpasses hers. Axiel was more than just a friend—his absence left a permanent emptiness within me, impossible to replace. "This isn't goodbye, it's bad-bye!"

Resting my head on his chest, my tears soaking his hospital garment as I sobbed, I became uncertain if it was merely my imagination and desperation, but I could faintly hear the rhythm of his heartbeat, starting with an intermittent thump before gradually growing stronger. His hand gently touched mine, and I immediately felt the comforting warmth that radiated from his touch as I glanced up at him. As his eyes slowly opened, I caught a fleeting glimpse of violet before they settled into their usual amber-hazel color.

"Axiel?" I called with a sniffle

He forced me a smile, "Have I ever told you that you have the most beautiful *gray* eyes I've ever seen?"

"He's alive?" his mother gasped, her voice filled with disbelief. "How is that possible?"

"Axiel, you're all—" my words were abruptly silenced as the world around me dissolved into an abyss of darkness.

CHAPTER FIFTEEN

SEE US TOGETHER

A FEW DAYS LATER
VYOLETTE

I awake, feeling the comforting warmth that I had grown accustomed to. Opening my eyes, I blinked a few times until the familiar surroundings of Axiel's parents' home came into focus. Axiel's touch sent a warm sensation through my hand, and when I glanced over, his joyful expression filled my sight.

"Welcome back," he smiled

Tears streamed down my face as I threw myself at him, tightly hugging him. "Axiel, I thought I had lost you," I cried in a cracked voice.

"I thought I was a goner too," he replied, "but then I woke up and saw you," He explained to me how, after being pulled back to his physical body, he was met with the chaotic sounds of the hospital room as the doctors pronounced him dead a few minutes later. He desperately attempted to return to me, yet he found himself confined within an unseen barrier. Lost in a void, he believed he was trapped until my voice reached his ears. He claimed he saw me materialize before him in said void, my voice echoing in his ears, pleading with him not to abandon me. He added, I placed my hand over my chest and pulled out a bright orb, which he eagerly accepted when I handed it to him. "And next thing I knew, I awakened to the sight of you," he concluded

I couldn't recall anything he was saying, the last thing I remembered was him disappearing in my arms the night of prom when we were back here. No matter how much he explained, my only focus was holding him tighter, savoring the joy of being in his arms again as he held me close—I felt a sense of wholeness returning.

It turned out that I had been unconscious for a week, and his parents had me brought here so I could rest. They informed Axiel about my identity, a rare gem destined for the supernatural realm, and revealed that I was the reason they intended to abandon him for a year—they were on a mission to find me. Why? Well, they've been waiting for me to wake up so they could tell Axiel and me.

After changing into something more comfortable—a white t-shirt under a short plaid pinafore dress, Axiel and I made our way down the stairs to the lounge where his parents were waiting. "I'm not sure if you remember meeting them, but this is my mother, Jade," he said, gesturing towards a young woman with warm, amber-hazel eyes resembling his. "And my father, Scott," he continued, pointing to a tall man with a friendly smile.

"Nice to meet you," I said politely, reaching out a hand and shaking theirs gently.

"You truly don't remember us?" Jade questioned

"I'm sorry, but I don't," I replied.

They kindly asked me to sit down before we started our conversation. With a reassuring nod from Axiel, I took a seat across from his parents and he sat beside me, taking my hand in his. "There's not much we can tell you for now," his father stated, "but about eighteen years ago, when Axiel was born, we were given the news that his future had already been mapped out."

"How come?" I questioned confused, "What do you mean mapped out?"

"There hasn't been a boy born into my family for almost a century," Jade responded, "Apparently, Knightly isn't just a last name, it's a commitment to a special type of reap—individual,"

"Your kind," Scott added, "you in specific,"

"Me?" I pointed at myself, my mind consumed with confusion as his father nodded in agreement.

"Yes," he confirmed, adjusting himself in his seat. "You see, it's a haunting cycle that has plagued my wife's family for centuries. They would always give birth to a baby girl, but for a boy, it's always been the same grim reality—on the fourth month, they would endure labor and ultimately deliver a stillborn baby." he recounted, "When we discovered we were expecting a boy, my mother-in-law insisted we terminate the pregnancy to avoid the anguish and pain that was sure to follow. Nevertheless, my wife—your mother, stood firm in her decision to keep you, Axiel. We were fully aware of the destiny that awaited our child, mirroring the misfortune of his ancestors. Yet, against all odds, he defied expectations by coming into the world at just twenty weeks, proving himself a true fighter."

"How come?" I asked, showing a genuine interest and curiosity.

"Believe it or not, the doctors were ready to give up on him until he began wailing," she replied, "when I looked near the door I saw your mother, the doctor asked her what she was doing there and she said she was simply drawn to be in my delivery room. I felt like she saved Axiel that night—it was only later your grandmother and my mother explained to us you were the one who saved him,"

"They explained to us you and Axiel were bonded by fate and that he only survived to protect you since you were conceived around the same time," his father added, "males of the Knightly family are to be knights for the daughters of the White family when they turn eighteen—though we were supposed to keep you two apart to avoid the two of you being sucked into the supernatural realm,"

"Why?" Axiel questioned, "Is that why I was so drawn to her the day I first saw her?"

"We wished you had told us about it, son," his father commented, "when we heard of the accident, it was said that you died with your parents, but a few months ago, we got wind that you were alive and were ordered to find you,"

"By whom?" I questioned, "The people who killed my parents and tried killing me, too?"

"No," his mother responded sternly, "it doesn't matter anymore, you and Axiel are now fully connected, the only thing we can do now is to prepare you for your 21st birthday, Vyolette,"

"What happens on her 21st birthday?" Axiel questioned, his brow furrowed in confusion.

"You will know when the time comes," his father cryptically replied, "but for now, we rely on you to protect her and train her."

Axiel stared at his parents confused, "train her?"

"Yes, train her," his father insisted, "we have a feeling—though she has no memory of it—Vyolette had something to do with you coming back to life after the doctors pronounced you dead, and she may have given you some of her abilities, so you will need to train her to use hers until all her powers fully awakened, on her 21st birthday. They will come for her and she needs to be prepared by then,"

"You're not making any sense, Dad," Axiel argued, frustration evident in his voice.

His father let out a tired sigh. "We know," he replied, getting to his feet, "we'll talk to the higher-ups, until then we'll need you two to go back to her parents' lake house and stay safe—you shouldn't be bothered up there."

"My parents' lake house?" I said, confused, "You mean the lake house where Axiel and I—"

"Stayed before the prom," Axiel shouted, his voice echoing through the room, before regaining his composure and continuing, "where we stayed for the entire week prior to that unfortunate incident at prom?"

"Yes," his mother eyed him strangely, "there's a special ward on there placed by her grandmother—"

"Axiel," I stated, my confusion palpable, "I thought that was your lake house..."

With a scoff, his mother couldn't help but laugh, her laughter carrying a light and amused tone. "We're rich, but we're not that rich sweetheart," she laughed, "That entire area belongs to your family—well as the sole survivor of your parents, it all belongs to you,"

"But I'm not rich," I retaliated, "my parents were average—"

"It's no surprise, considering your family practically controls the organization and you have almost five times the money we do," she interjected, "To protect you, they had to conceal their wealth,"

Axiel's parents were cautious in their conversation, providing me with just enough information to leave me feeling puzzled and inquisitive.

➔ANOTHER WEEK LATER

Graduation went off without a hitch, even though I had worried about potential issues stemming from prom night. Axiel's parents, who I suspected played a role, ensured everything went smoothly. With every step I took toward the stage to collect my diploma, I could feel a deep realization that my parents were there, their presence comforting and reassuring.

We all celebrated with a dinner at a luxurious, upscale restaurant. The private area added an intimate touch, and as we laughed and shared stories, I finally felt a sense of belonging, like I was part of a family again. During that dinner, his parents insisted we delay college for a few years so that I could gain complete mastery over my dormant powers. My eyes have fully regained their natural gray color, and I haven't encountered any lost or wandering souls since I woke up. However, his parents warned me that if I lived without control over my emotions and what I could do, my eyes could easily turn violet again or even white if I became too angry or emotional.

ↆ...

Axiel walked over to me, his footsteps echoing softly on the pavement, and pulled me into a warm embrace. He planted a gentle kiss on my cheek, all while his parents stood on the front porch, waving at us with wide smiles. "Ready to go?" he asked, his eyes sparkling with enthusiasm as he closed the trunk of his new low orange, 5-seater Ford Ranger pickup truck.

I nodded in agreement, "Yeah—I looked back at his home—I won't lie, I'm gonna miss this place,"

His voice dripping with flirtation, Axiel whispered in my ear, making me quiver. "But you're gonna love the lake house even more since we're gonna have it all to ourselves and I am *physically* here now,"

I playfully gave him a gentle shove before settling into the passenger seat of the car and buckling up. He hopped into the car, secured his seatbelt, and smoothly pulled out of the driveway, exchanging brief conversations as we cruised into town. Our first stop was the main supermarket—***Mega G's***, where we filled our carts with an abundance of groceries in bulk, preparing ourselves for the next few months.

"Axiel, do you think we should stop at the pet shop for a pet?" I posed the question, imagining how delightful it would be to have a canine or feline companion join us at the lake house.

"Hmm… well—"

"Well, well, well..." said a very familiar voice, dripping with sarcasm. "If it isn't ghost girl and her loyal pet."

Glancing in the corner of my eye, I saw Rejanae and her group of shit-stains approaching us, Britney standing with her arms folded tightly across her chest, shooting us a piercing glare. Despite Rejanae's friendly greeting to him, Axiel completely disregarded her and deliberately veered our carts away, avoiding any interaction with the group.

Cody and Kelly, their faces red with anger, abruptly rushed in front of us, forcefully pushing our cart backward and halting our progress. "I don't care about what Mr. Jakins claims," Cody spat, "but what went down at that prom was definitely not some damn staged show!"

Axiel's voice was filled with barely contained anger as he uttered, "Get out of our way, or else I will make you," careful to keep his voice low so as not to disturb the other customers nearby.

Cody's mischievous smirk grew wider as he swiftly plucked a couple of boxes from our cart, releasing them onto the ground with a loud thud before proceeding to stomp on them, filling the aisle with a cacophony of sounds.

"We're not in high school anymore!" I barked at them, frustrated, "Grow the hell up!"

"C'mon Vyolette," said Axiel, holding me by my waist, "We can drive uptown to a different store."

Leaving the carts abandoned in the aisle, we made our way towards the front door. Rejanae trailed behind us, and suddenly she rushed ahead, shoving me forcefully backward. Thankfully, Axiel's tight grip kept me steady. "You took everything from me!" she growled, her voice filled with anger. "Axiel should be with me!"

Remembering what his parents had said after I woke up, I couldn't help but scoff, finding Rejanae's words amusing. Axiel's entire purpose in life was to be by my side, his presence a testament to our unbreakable bond—but he's with me because we have a love that he willingly and passionately chose. "Let's go Axiel," I said, wrapping my arm under his.

He agreed and stepped up to Rejanae, "I never loved you," he said sternly, "I loved the idea of loving you—and there is no way I'd ever be interested in someone with a heart as cold, and black as yours. Never bother me or Vyolette again, or I swear I will make sure you and your family live a life you could never comprehend!"

Her eyes shimmered with tears and her body trembled as we walked by her. In an instant, I sensed a forceful blow to the back of my head, the impact of the object that hit me resonating with a distinct thud as it fell to the floor. Feeling the impact where I was hit, I examined the faint smudge of blood on my fingertips before turning around to confront her.

With a growl, my anger surged through me, intensifying with each passing second. "What the hell is your problem?"

With a loud shout, she bared her soul in confession. "Before I set fire to that goddamn house, I should have made sure you were asleep!"

"You!" I snarled, "You were the one who burned my home down!"

There was an intense, electrifying sensation flowing through me, but it dissipated as soon as Axiel's gentle touch provided comfort. Taking advantage of the moment, Rejanae quickly snatched another tin from the shelf and hurled it towards me. As I cowered, bracing for impact, I felt the reassuring presence of Axiel's arm around me. I slowly opened my eyes and gazed up at him, mesmerized by the violet glow in his eyes, a color I hadn't seen when I looked in a mirror for quite some time. His other hand was raised, and to my surprise, the can was suspended in mid-air, just inches away from us.

'Was this what his parents told him I'm capable of doing?' I questioned in thought.

The can crashed onto the cold marble floor, embedding itself in the marble, and shattering around it into fragments with a force that seemed to defy gravity. Rejanae's eyes locked with his intense gaze, causing her to involuntarily retreat and inadvertently sweep the nearby shelf, sending groceries cascading to the ground. "What the fuck is wrong with your eyes—" she cried

"I warned you to leave us be!" Axiel growled, "You and your friends need to be taught a lesson,"

The shelves trembled as more objects took flight, filling the room with a cacophony of crashing sounds. In response, they screamed in terror and sought comfort in each other's arms as they tried hiding behind our abandoned carts. Noticing Axiel becoming uneasy, I swiftly interjected by resting my hand on his chest, silently imploring him to stop and calm down. We were in a supermarket and the last thing I wanted at the moment was to draw attention to us—after all, we were leaving the town for a while and we didn't have to come back here when it was time to buy more groceries and necessities.

"Axiel, please stop!" I cried, my words choked with emotion. "They're not worth it!"

With a swift motion, he lowers his hand, and the sound of objects hitting the ground echoes through the air. Rejanae and her friends hastily jumped up and dashed out of the store, their terrified screams filling the air as they referred to Axiel and me as "freaks."

"Unless they want to find themselves in an insane asylum, they should stay quiet about what just happened," Axiel stated, leading me out of the store and back to the pickup. "We'll stop at the mega-mall at the edge of town to get what we need—I'll call my parents to deal with this and the security footage."

He called his parents, and as he expected, they assured him they would handle the situation involving Rejanae and her friends. As much as I would love to see them rot in jail for burning my home down and fully taking my parents away from me, Axiel said it wasn't worth the hassle and to stop looking back, and to only look forward.

We made a stop at the mega-mall, where we stocked up on groceries, toiletries, clothing, and a few essential pieces of equipment before continuing on our route to the lake house. After witnessing the tumultuous scene at Mega G's, I couldn't shake the sense that the time Axiel and I would be spending up there for the next three years would be filled with challenges.

ABOUT THE AUTHOR

KIA Valcent is an author born on the small Caribbean Island of Saint Lucia who writes novellas and novels of various genres such as Romance, Mystery, Teen-Fiction, Supernatural (Vampire/Werewolves/Demons/Zombies), Sci-Fi, Crime, Paranormal, Young Adult Fiction, Non-Fiction, and Fantasy Fiction (Mermaids/Magic/Superpowers) with a slice-of-life. She stepped into the world of self-publishing in June 2021, under her business DarkRoyalty Books.

She wrote her first book, A Daughter's Nightmare when she was 11 years old to help cope with her trauma. There is still a lot she must learn about writing, editing, publishing, and being an author, and is already taking the steps to learn it all. For her, there is always room for improvement.

With an insatiable desire to put her thoughts on paper, KIA is easily inspired to write a story by the simplest of things (an image, song, word, or video clip). She started at a very young age and was told to share her stories on Wattpad by her dear friend J. Joseph in April 2018. There, she developed an audience and improved her writing with each book she wrote.

With the encouragement of her mother and sister, she took to the self-publishing world, hoping to be a well-known author in her country someday.

Follow KIA Valcent on Twitter
https://twitter.com/KiaValcent

Follow DarkRoyalty Books on TikTok
https://www.tiktok.com/@darkroyaltybooks

Follow DarkRoyalty Books on Facebook
https://www.facebook.com/DarkRoyaltyBooks

Follow DarkRoyalty Books on Instagram
https://www.instagram.com/DarkRoyaltyBooks

DarkRoyalty Books Website
https://darkroyaltybooks.wixsite.com/kiavalcent

Milton Keynes UK
Ingram Content Group UK Ltd.
UKHW010642080724
445166UK00001B/24